In the blacked-out carriage of a train running through "unoccupied" France sits a young American girl, Fenton Ravel. She knows that two men share her compartment, but in the blackness she cannot see their faces. As the night wears on, the two men try to draw her into conversation—to discover what brings her alone into this dangerous country. But Fenton is too wary to speak the words aloud to strangers—that she has come to search for her lover, Bastineau, who was swallowed up in the dark intrigues that followed the coming of the enemy.

In the morning the train arrives at the little Alpine village of Truex. Then the nightmare quality of Fenton's journey really begins. Here, where she has spent many joyous holidays, Fenton finds herself frozen out by the hostility of her old friends. Conversations cease at her approach. When she mentions the name of Bastineau, begging for word of him, heads turn away. The entire will of the village seems concentrated in one desperate purpose—to get her out of Truex, and at once.

Even more ominous is the constant presence of the two men who traveled with her in the blacked-out train. Wherever Fenton turns, they are at hand: De Vaudois, the imperious Swiss with the cold intelligent eyes and the scar on his cheek; and Jacqueminot, the faunlike young Frenchman, a newcomer to the village. Whether they mean to help her or destroy her she cannot tell.

Fenton's love for Bastineau forces her to continue her search for him. She ignores the warning of the guides who intimate that for anyone seeking Bastineau death waits in the mountains.

Finally, on a dangerous Alpine trail, roped to the man whom she now recognizes as an enemy, Fenton solves the mystery of Bastineau's disappearance. On her courage and fast thinking rests the safety of the entire village and of a vital link in the French underground.

Avalanche is a tale of danger and courage. At the same time it is a richly emotional love story, with a hero to remember.

Avalanche

Avalanche

a novel by KAY BOYLE

1944 — Simon and Schuster, New York

THIS BOOK HAS NOT BEEN CONDENSED. ITS BULK
IS LESS BECAUSE GOVERNMENT REGULATIONS
PROHIBIT USE OF HEAVIER PAPER.

MANUFACTURED IN THE UNITED STATES OF AMERICA

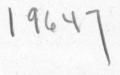

TO

Monsieur and Madame Rrose Sélavy

Avalanche

One

IN ONE compartment, set directly over the loud concussion of the wheels, there were three people traveling. They were strangers to one another, and they sat in three corners of the compartment in darkness, their coats drawn around them against the cold of the late October night. The train was the kind the French call an *omnibus*, which meant that it would grind lingeringly to a halt at every station of the line. But after two and a half years of defeat, express trains, upholstered seats, and dining cars were expected no longer. No one had foreseen, however, that, due to faulty wiring in the anti-

3

quated cars which the conquerors permitted the conquered to make use of still, the trip toward the mountains was to be made in darkness. But this too the passengers accepted. It was 1942, and the days of demands were temporarily done.

Only one of the three people in the compartment had boarded the train at the point of its departure, and that was the girl. The two men had opened the door at different halts beyond Lyon, and the girl had drawn her feet back to allow each of them to thrust his bags in before him in the dark and draw himself up into the unlighted car. The first man had lifted his bag with some difficulty, as if unaccustomed to doing such things for himself, and then manipulated himself up the high step and into the compartment, and past her to the farthest corner by the corridor. As he pushed past her, he had pronounced the correct word of apology to the darkness, and he sat down at the other end of the compartment, breathing hard, leaving on the air for a moment the smell of soap— fresh, fragrant soap—in a country where soap had long been a rarity.

Sitting there sleepless in her soft coat by the window, the girl believed she saw him clearly for an instant, and having seen him in her mind's eye she dismissed him as one of those thickset, stubbornly built men of no definable age who had acquired a lightness of step and delicacy of movement through nothing more than a strict and habitual practice of formality. The second man had joined them an hour or so later, swinging himself up from the platform with ease, and saying *"Pardon"* in quick concern to the sound of the girl's shifting

4

feet. Then he had placed himself in the corner opposite her, riding backward as the train jerked into motion again.

The girl had not yet been able to sleep, and now the presence of the second man disturbed her. In the months she had been back in France, she had schooled herself to quick, cool judgment of face and voice, and she listened while he shifted in impatience on the boards of the seat. He was not a city man, she thought, or a man accustomed to the duress of travel, and she sat with her coat drawn around her, staring before her into the dark as if to compel some picture of him to take shape upon the blankness there. Perhaps he was a peasant come in like this from a village on the plain and riding only a station or two farther; or he might, by some miracle, be a mountain man, she thought. He might even be a guide or a skier returning to the Mont Blanc range, a man down from a high mountain place who would know Bastineau, she thought in hope an instant. And then she stopped herself abruptly: once she had reached the mountains, it would be enough to find Bastineau, or what news of him there was, without asking that signs of him be given on the way.

And now the man she had not placed yet lowered the blackout curtain on the window, a relic of that immutable past when France had been at war, and it snapped free of his hand and spun loudly upward on its spool.

"*Pardon,*" he said again, but this time he went on speaking. "They might have left us a few decent *wagons* without violating the terms of the armistice," he said, his voice dismissing tragedy with the wry, flippant bitterness that could

5

come only from a Frenchman's tongue. "Except that any-thing with cushions on it might lead us into the mistaken be-lief that we are human beings still," he said, and she liked the sound of it.

For a moment there was nothing further said above the wheels' clamor and the straining timber's protest, but the sense of listening was drawn tight as a wire from corner to corner in the compartment's dark. It was everywhere in France now; it was present on every street, in every café, be-hind the counter of every shop. You closed yourself in a moving train, the girl thought, and it was with you still, the wheels beneath you admonishing: *Wait and listen, wait and listen. Do not speak the name of any man or destination, no matter how hot and urgent the words are that want to be said.* And then the other man in the farthest corner by the corridor yawned aloud.

"This taking of the biggest and best for their own require-ments serves a double purpose," he said, beginning it as casually as if he had turned at a dinner table to include the seated company as he spoke. "They get the superior matériel," he said, "and at the same time they accustom the defeated population to a rolling stock more appropriate to its condi-tion." And *They*, thought the girl, *is no longer a pronoun. In the time I have been away, it has come to be the exact refer-ence made to only one nation of men.* "I've been traveling in both zones, the Occupied as well as this one," the man said out of the dark, "and it is a system that has its points. It keeps the national pride of a conquered country in its proper place." As he spoke, the girl came to another decision. *He is not a French-*

6

man, she thought, and she sat there with her coat drawn close around her. *That is not a Frenchman's accent or a Frenchman's mind.*

"There's enough going on to keep my national pride alive for the moment," said the man sitting opposite her, and he seemed to shift in impatience on his seat. The quality of his voice was good, and the quality of his restlessness like that of an animal habituated to freedom who refuses, viciously and savagely, to be confined.

"Well, then let me prove the same point by taking the Americans," said the other man in a leisurely voice from the corner where he sat. "If you should take an American's skyscrapers, and his Clippers, and all his childish, mammoth displays away from him, you would be depriving him of the props of his self-respect. Surround a man with poor equipment, and naturally his standards deteriorate." The rising tumult of the wheels beneath them as they took a curve silenced his voice an instant, and then he asked sardonically: "Would you say we broke an axle that time?"

"No," said the other man in quick, bitter pride. "Even antiquated French matériel somehow holds together. It's a phenomenon only Frenchmen understand."

"It cracked up badly enough two years ago," said the man in the far corner, and then the girl heard the Frenchman opposite her say the single, blasphemous word beneath his breath. "But the French remain an interesting subject," the man's voice went on, and again they heard him yawn. "If you prefer, I'm quite willing to put the Americans aside for the moment——"

7

It was now, for the first time, that the girl spoke.

"I'm afraid I can't allow you to put the Americans aside," she said, and her voice was young and reckless in the dark of the careening car.

The Frenchman did not stir on the wooden seat, and the man in the far corner did not yawn again. For an instant after she had spoken there was nothing to be heard except the clamor of the unevenly revolving wheels, and then the man sitting at the other end of the compartment laughed. It was a startled and not unpleasant laugh.

"You are a long way from home, *mademoiselle*," he said urbanely, but however light the tone of his voice was, the entire darkness was waiting. The compartment was one wide, harking ear.

"This is home," the girl said, and the same young, reckless quality was in the sound of it. "Only my mother was American. My father is French."

She heard the Frenchman shift on the seat opposite her now, and when he spoke, his voice had altered in wonder or curiosity.

"You speak the language without an accent," he said.

"I was brought up in these mountains," the girl said, and there was another moment of quiet as the two men listened in separate speculation to the voice, the eternal listening for commitment still sharp on the air. "That is, whenever I could get away from school," she said, and it may have been that they saw for an instant in the returning dark the wide-spaced eyes, and the upturned nose, and the pigtails hanging as they must have hung on her shoulders only a little while ago.

8

"Do you smoke, *mademoiselle?*" asked the Frenchman quickly. For a moment she believed she could see the hand, weathered and young, the nails on it blunted from rock or soil or from whatever work he did, holding the flattened packet toward her across the dark.

"I used to—when cigarettes came easily," she said.

"I have three left," said the Frenchman, as eagerly and generously as Bastineau might have said it, but still she did not put out her hand.

"Keep them," she said. "They'll go quickly enough."

"I'm afraid she's seen through you," said the man in the other corner, and he laughed again. "Of course, you, being French, *monsieur*, are curious about her looks. Is she twenty or thirty, you are asking yourself. If you struck a match, that much would be settled. But I assure you that all American women are young and beautiful on principle. Far more interesting that she doesn't smoke, for then these false faces we are wearing would be removed to give place to our own."

The wheels ground on beneath them, and the girl sat wide-eyed in the darkness, looking straight ahead to where the Frenchman must be. *If you come from the mountains,* she wanted to say aloud to him, *you may know a man called Bastineau. He has quick black eyes and hair the right color, and he always climbs rocks or glaciers singing aloud. There was the spring when I was fourteen, and we climbed a long way on foot that April, and the crocuses were coming up through the lacy islands that were left of the winter's snow. And I fell into the high mountain pond where last year's frog corpses floated pure as lilies, and I saw the spiked mountain*

9

boot on the bright new grass as I fell, and the wool of his stocking, and the buckle strapping the dark trouser just below the knee. But I didn't see the hand that pulled me out by the belt until it was wiping my face dry with the red cotton handkerchief taken off his own neck. He picked the water cress, or whatever it was, out of my hair the way you take burrs from a filly's stubborn tail, and he didn't laugh. When we got back to the chalet, I wrote it down indelibly forever. I wrote: "When I was fourteen and fell into the frog pond, Bastineau didn't laugh at me."

"So here the three of us are," the man in the farthest corner was saying, "apparently closed in together for the night. Not only shall we doubtless never see one another again, but we have the added interest of never having seen one another. If we were quite certain that we were all going separate ways before dawn, we could pass the time by telling the stories of our lives. Probably quite diverse experiences in national pride. Now I, being Swiss, am partial to the virtues of neutrality——"

"If you're on your way back to Switzerland, perhaps I could trouble you to send a few things back from your side of the frontier," said the Frenchman's voice ironically. "I'd like, for instance, a few dozen pairs of mountain boots, sealskins, ice skates, snowshoes, and a selection of hickory skis and metal ski poles——"

"Defeated populations," said the Swiss from his corner, "can scarcely deal in luxuries."

"I have a sport shop in a winter resort," the Frenchman went on rather bitterly. "It wouldn't be a bad shop if I had anything in it to sell. I've been down here on the plain trying to find something in the way of stock, but there's nothing left to buy. I managed to pick up a little wool—not pure wool, God knows, but something good enough to be knitted into skiers' mittens for next winter's trade. With their usual efficiency, they've cleaned us systematically out," he said.

There was the winter when the white horse started coming to the chalet window in the evening, went the girl's unspoken conversation with the Frenchman opposite in the dark. *He would come up the road no matter how deep the snow was, making his own tracks in the moonlight or starlight, with the frost shining like crystals in his mane. He did not come out of love, but for sugar and apple halves, and he ate them through the kitchen window, with the icicles melting from his lips and nostrils in the heat from the stove. I wanted to catch the horse and ride him, but Bastineau said to wait until the spring when the ground was soft to do it—I waited till February, which is the peasants' spring. I got the bridle and bit from the back of the harness shop, and I put it on him one night while his head was through the window, and I rode him bareback down through the pines. He was shy of the road because of the shape of the rocks with the thaw streaming on them, and he reared on his heels and soared like an angel across me when I fell. And suddenly there were arms in a jacket around me, lifting me and taking me home, and I could not stop the sound of my voice from saying: "Bastineau, I love you. I love you, Bastineau." I was fifteen that year, and I died of shame every time I remembered it after. When I passed that place in the road skiing or walking, my heart grew weak, but Bastineau*

II

*never looked back or gave any sign that he might be thinking:
"That's where you made a fool of yourself the night the white
horse threw you. That's where you made a declaration of love
to me when I found you lying there."*

The train had come to a stop now in a station which was
more than merely a village halt, and the passengers in the
other compartments opened the carriage doors and, as if groping their way from sleep, got down upon the platform and
moved numbly off beneath the hooded lights. Their baskets
and bags hung from their hands, and their shoulders were
stooped by the weight of them as they moved in silence, free
men no longer, walking wearily toward the station door as the
doomed and shackled walk.

"This is the last stop before we begin climbing," the Frenchman said, and the Swiss, seated in the corner with his coat
around him still, took his watch from his pocket and looked
at the phosphorescent numerals on its face.

"Twenty minutes past two," he said.

The light from the station fell in broken fragments through
the train windows now and partially lit the compartment, and
in its dimness the girl saw the Frenchman opposite take on
tentative and momentary shape. He was leaning toward her,
the packet of cigarettes in his hand—a slender, quick-gestured
man, with a boyish, eager turn to his dark head. The thick,
lumberjack shirt was open at the neck, and his throat was bare
as a mountaineer's would be.

"There are still three cigarettes left, *mademoiselle*," he
said, and, as if establishing a bond between them, she took
one from his hand. At once the match's flame was there, held

12

carefully and steadily for her, and the Frenchman's eyes, sober and dark, were on her face.

And now the Swiss got to his feet, and he came forward, holding his coat around him, and stooped to take a light as well from the match held in the Frenchman's hand. His eyes were bright, sharp, and cold above his hard, pink cheeks as he examined her briefly and exactly, and then he looked with the same precision at the features of the Frenchman's face.

"Thank you," he said with satisfaction as the match went out. Now that he had them fixed, marked indelible as a thumbprint on the eye's retina, he turned back to his corner in the darkness and sat down. "We gentlemen have given a certain account of ourselves," he said as he drew the first deep breath of smoke in, "but the third point of the triangle is still obscure. Why a beautiful young lady with an American mother should be traveling through France, at night, alone——"

The train had begun to move out of the station, the turning wheels crying out shrilly beneath them on the track. The Swiss yawned over his cigarette, crossed his legs, and leaned back as if in preparation for sleep, and the lights from the station fell in white spokes across their faces before they moved again into the utter dark.

"I belong here," the girl said, smoking. "I got back to France a month ago. I've climbed these glaciers and skied down these trails year after year. I know the Mont Blanc range like the palm of my hand," she said, and she heard the Frenchman say it. "Bravo, bravo," he said softly to the dark.

There was one winter when the blizzard got us part way up, went the unspoken conversation with him. *If you looked in the direction the wind was coming from, your breath stopped suddenly as if someone took you by the throat. Bastineau was ahead, breaking the way with skins strapped to his skis, but no matter how close you kept, his tracks were wiped out before you could catch up with him. We'd been going two hours, and Bastineau said: "When we get to the cornice, we'll break the cattle refuge in and slap each other's backs to warm our hands, and kick our feet into life again." And we did this: we stood our skis upright outside the hut, and Bastineau took off his leather mittens, and the second pair inside, and he rubbed my hands until I cried with the pain. He slapped my cheeks twice to make the blood come back in them again, and then he said: "Fenton—Fenton, it's crazy." I was seventeen that year, and that was the first time we kissed each other. When he had kissed me like that, he said: "Put on your mittens," as if he were sending me back to school. He picked his own gloves up from where they were, like the hands of a statue broken off in the cold. Then he walked out the door ahead of me into the blizzard again, and he stooped and strapped my skis on for me.*

"Have you been away a long time?" the Swiss was saying from his corner.

"Three years," the girl said quietly. "When the war broke here, the family took me back to America. I was eighteen then, and I had to be obedient. Now I'm doing what I always wanted to do."

The second time he kissed me was the day France declared war, she did not say aloud in the darkness. *He kissed me as*

14

solemnly and terribly as if he put a ring on my finger that I would wear forever.

"So you're the advance guard of the second front?" said the Swiss, and he laughed his not-unpleasant laugh. "Perhaps we should notify the proper authorities that an American has landed," he said, and the Frenchman said the same short, blasphemous word beneath his breath again.

"I'm working in Lyon with a relief committee," the girl said. "We distribute vitamins and powdered milk—bought in your country, by the way. I've been working a bit hard at it, so my chairman told me to clear out and take a fortnight's holiday." And *Don't say the name of the town,* she admonished herself in silence. *Don't ask the Frenchman if he's ever been to Truex, or if he knows a man named Bastineau.* Aloud, she said: "So I took the first train for the mountains."

"I've done some mountain climbing and skiing around here myself," said the Swiss from his corner.

"It's not easy to get the permission to do it now," the Frenchman said.

"Mountain climbing," said the Swiss, "is what I've come here to do. Only, this time there's rather a sinister twist to it." From the note in his voice now, it might have been a confidence he was approaching, and the girl and the Frenchman waited for the rest of it to come. "There was rather a serious accident in August of this year," the Swiss went on, "just below the Mont Maudit."

"Yes," said the Frenchman, as if he were on his own ground at last. "Yes, that is true."

15

"There was an avalanche that caught a young mountain climber and his guide as they crossed a slope above the ice cliffs. Their bodies were never found."

"Yes," said the Frenchman again. "I was in the first search party that set out. I come from Truex," and at the sound of the name spoken, the girl leaned suddenly forward in the dark. "The avalanche came down between twelve and two o'clock. It was seen through the telescope from the Hôtel de la Gare. We started out at once, but it took eight hours to get there. We worked all that night by moonlight, trying to get them out." His voice as he said these things was quiet, as if tempered by the mountains' height, and cold, and the mountains' moonlit stillness. "We rested a bit when the dawn shift came on, and then we dug all day at the mass of snow."

"That was August," said the Swiss from the dark. "This is October. That boy is somewhere under there still."

"And the guide," the Frenchman said.

For a moment it seemed they might hear the Swiss yawn again, and then he apparently stifled it, for the voice went leisurely on:

"He came up from Geneva on vacation. I know his father well. I don't know if I mentioned that I'm in the watch and jewelry business—my factory just outside Geneva. So I've come here on a sort of sacred mission. I told that dead boy's father I'd stop off at Truex on my way home from this business trip to Paris, and that I'd find the boy's remains and take them back to Switzerland."

"It's a bad time of year for it," said the Frenchman. "And unless you have the proper papers, you may have some trouble.

The terms of the armistice between France and Italy have declared this region a military zone."

"The Swiss," said the other man from his corner, "are granted the special protection of providence because of their neutrality."

It was six o'clock in the morning when the train stopped at its final halt, not as if reaching a terminus, but more as if giving up in final exhaustion there. The passengers left in it got down from it in the early-morning light, their coats buttoned up against what might have been the icy air of winter. There they stood, a bleak, weary handful of men and women with hope desiccated in them, waiting for the electric train that would bear them higher on the last lap of the climb. They were not many to mount the steps of it: the Swiss, tall, heavy, and seal-headed, in a velvet-trimmed, city overcoat, a man of forty-five or fifty, settling himself into the last car alone; a few black-clad peasant women and men, some with their thin-legged, dark-eyed children with them, carrying baskets of what poor produce they had gleaned in a visit to the plain. They were not a festive people, nor were they a complaining people, but a people stricken by defeat who climbed into the summery-looking excursion train and seated themselves in silence on its wooden seats. There were no tourists, no pigskin luggage, no hastening, fur-clad women laughing and calling out from car to car as there had been in other years. The girl, her single bag in her hand, walked up the platform alone, mounted behind the electric engine, and sat down in the first car and combed out her smooth, light hair. When she had blotted out the night's fatigue with fresh lip rouge and powder, she looked up from her mirror and saw that the Frenchman had come into the same car with her and was swinging his rucksack up onto the rack above him just ahead. She watched him in quiet speculation a moment while he pushed the loaded rucksack into place: he was tall, and his shoulders were broad, and his ears lay pointed, faunlike, against the close, dark cap of crinkly hair. The reddish, flannel shirt was open at the neck, and he wore climbing knickerbockers and white knitted hose. Just before the train slid into motion, he turned and looked at her, and she saw the color rise suddenly in his face.

Piece by piece the train bore them upward through the canyons of rock and pine, and then without warning, on the right, the steepness of the narrow gorge opened as brilliantly as if someone had flung back the shutters in a darkened room. And there were the glaciers, the high, perilous staircases of ice, with the rich light of morning streaming on them. Almost at once, then, the smooth, unblemished shoulder of Mont Blanc rose against the slate-colored sky, and below its pure snows fell the carved flights of ice with the radiance of the sun pouring warm as wine across their clarity.

"They are just the same!" the girl cried out in wonder at the sight. "Nothing has changed, nothing!" And in the moment that she said it, it seemed to her that the men whose lives were passed in the presence of these eternally unaltering things might have survived defeat unaltered too.

The Frenchman had got to his feet now, and he stood looking through the window at the miracle of the heights unfolding, peak by cold, still peak above the twilit world.

"There are changes," he said. "For one thing, there is another Italy on the other side of these mountains now." He leaned his sun-bronzed hands on the two sides of the car window's frame. His nose was short and his upper lip was long, and out of the open collar of his shirt, his throat curved strong and muscular and brown. "If you were here three years ago, Italy was a possible ally then," he said. "We used to say to one another: 'The two Latin sisters need never fall out.'"

"I remember hearing that," the girl said. "All the years I lived here with my people, we used to say in Truex that mountain men, even if frontiers lay between them, were bound by ties that nothing could break."

"But that didn't save us from war," he said quickly. "Not even the same church, or the same warmth in our blood, was enough to bind her to us." Now that they were alone in the car, the talk came without vigilance between them. The Swiss was gone, and the night was gone, and the harking ear waited no longer for secret statement in the presence of the bold, cold mountains and the sun. "You do not speak of the mountains as a foreigner would," the Frenchman said. "You speak of them the way we do." His wrists, supporting his weight against the window still, were slight and flexible and hard as steel. "I come from the Petit St. Bernard," he said, "and I know the Italians well. We lived on the pass until the war broke out, and then we opened this sport shop in Truex. My mother opened it, that is, to keep herself and my sisters while the men of the family were away."

Then perhaps you knew Bastineau, the girl began it again in silence; *perhaps you've seen him skiing down fast in win-*

ter through the pine trees, or walking up fast in summer, alive like that as if life were a special honor given to only a few men in each generation who knew what to do with it once it was theirs. Perhaps you knew him up there, she did not say aloud, *a man who would look at a sunrise before he'd look at any woman, and who liked the taste of altitude better than any wine. Perhaps you could tell me if they got him at Dunkirk, if they put him away in prison camp with the two million other Frenchmen who are there, or if they merely wiped out his heart and his hope and let him go on living just the same. He wouldn't have had any use for death,* she could not say to the Frenchman; *he wouldn't know what to do with death, death wouldn't suit him at all.* And sitting there with the mountains growing tall around them, she felt the tears stand suddenly hot and helpless in her eyes.

"I've been wondering whom you climbed the glaciers with," the Frenchman said, as he watched the country through the window. "We mountain men know one another by name, or because we've done the heights together."

The girl brought her hands together under the gray-blue folds of her soft coat, and her nails cut into her palms as she looked straight out into the distant glacier's blaze.

"I climbed them with my father, most of them," she began, trying to say it easily. "There were guides, too—sometimes one, sometimes another." She was silent a moment, her hands pressed tightly together inside her coat, and then she said: "There was one guide we knew very well. We knew him for years here—a man called Bastineau."

The Frenchman did not speak at once, and when he did she

turned her head quickly at the altered sound of his voice, and she saw that the thing had happened to his face as well. Not only had the color gone from beneath the sunburned skin, but the features had contracted, the youth of the face had sharpened abruptly with what might have been wariness or what might have been merely pain.

"Yes, Bastineau," he said then. "Yes, I knew him."

She sat with her hands closed tight beneath her coat, watching the side of the Frenchman's face, the concave cheek, the delicate line of the jaw in which the pulse beat nervously.

"Please," she said in a low voice to the pointed ear, and to the eye that did not falter as it watched the rising heights of snow. "Whatever happened to him, I should like to know it. Frenchmen were killed, Frenchmen were taken prisoner ———" She felt her tightly clenched hands as cold as ice in her coat, and suddenly she cried out: "Why are we speaking of him in the past tense like this? Why did you say, 'Yes, I *knew* Bastineau?'"

He did not speak at once, and his eyes watched steadily through the car window's glass.

"How well did you know Bastineau?" he asked.

"I grew up with him," she said quite simply. And now the Frenchman turned his head, and his dark eyes met hers in singularly exacting gravity. He looked at her in silence, and then he turned back to the window, and there was the mark of pain again around his mouth and eyes.

"You won't find Bastineau in Truex," he said after a moment. "That's all we know. There isn't any grave to put flowers on, or any address to write to. I suppose we might just

21

as well call it 'missing,' " he said, his voice as gentle as a woman's as he said the words.

The train had slid quietly into the mountain station now, and the name of Truex was called aloud. As they came to a halt, the Frenchman lifted his rucksack down and thrust his arms through the straps of it and shook it into place on his back. Then he stooped by her seat and took the girl's bag in his hand.

"You mean—he didn't come back?" she said quickly to him.

"Yes," said the Frenchman. He was standing close to her in the car's aisle, tall and lean, his face in profile with the eyebrow tipped, faunlike, to the temple, and the pulse beating quickly in his jaw. "He didn't come back," he said.

They crossed the familiar square in silence, past the stone water trough where she had watched the cattle come in other years to drink, past the monument standing to the village's war dead. Whatever questions might have been asked and answers given were hushed now by one man's absence which lay like the weight of the dead between them. The Frenchman, with his pack on his shoulders, went into the Hôtel de la Gare before her, and set her bag down by the desk.

"You'll remember Madame Perrin," he said as he touched the bell on the counter. Then he looked at the girl standing there in her soft blue coat, and his eyes faltered a moment before the look of young, shocked benumbment in her face. But Madame Perrin stood behind the counter now, and when he had greeted her, he shifted the rucksack on his back. "I have brought you a client," he said, and then he went, slender and

22

light, the hips narrow, the shoulders broad, down the length of the hotel hallway and out the open door.

The girl watched him go, the sense of bereavement quickening in her, and then she turned to the hotel desk and spoke to the woman who stood behind it.

"You're looking thinner, Madame Perrin," she said, and the woman started at the sound of her voice, and leaned forward on the wood.

"Mademoiselle Ravel!" she cried, breathing it scarcely aloud. "It's Mademoiselle Ravel!" She reached across the counter, and their hands closed on each other's. *Once*, thought Fenton, *there was some bitter question of finances between us. Once there were extra bottles of wine slipped on to bills for dinners we ate here, or for apéritifs we hadn't had. Once I could see nothing but the cold look of acquisition in her face, but war and defeat and a common cause have given other dimensions to us.* "Yes, yes," Madame Perrin was saying, "we are all thinner, the whole nation is thinner. But you have come from a better country. *Dieu*, you are beautiful! So well fed, *mademoiselle*, and the coat real wool!"

Behind Madame Perrin, a mirror hung the width of the wall, and, as if suddenly perceiving two strangers in the room, Fenton looked up at the reflection of herself and the hotel proprietress in its glass. She saw the woman's middle-aged back, and the waves of black hair set on her head, and, facing her, a girl in a gray-blue coat with the soft collar of it buttoned against her throat, and the shoulders broad and military. The girl's head was bare, the hair light and long and combed smoothly back behind the ears; the mouth in the oval, pure

23

white face was coral, and the wide-set eyes that watched her were singularly grim.

"And your husband?" she said to Madame Perrin, and she saw the lips of the girl in the mirror move stiffly as she spoke the words. Then her eyes left the glass and returned to the reality of the quarter inch of white which bordered Madame Perrin's brow where the dye no longer touched the roots.

"Gustav was eight months a prisoner," the Frenchwoman said. She was looking in wonder still at Fenton. "Three of them escaped together. He has his old place back at the post office now. And you! You've come back like our prisoners," Madame Perrin said. "Perhaps it's a sign that the tide is turning when our prisoners and the Americans return."

The room would be the one with the balcony facing the mountain range, and they went up the narrow stairs to it, and Madame Perrin flung open the shutters to the light of day. There was Mont Blanc again, this time almost perpendicular from the outskirts of the town, and the glaciers close enough, it seemed, to reach out and touch with the hand. Fenton walked out onto the balcony, and behind her in the bedroom, Madame Perrin set the cloth on the dresser straight, adjusted a chair, blew the dust from the table, thumped the pillows on the bed.

"It's been empty a long time," she was saying in complaint. "There are not so many tourists now. Of course, in the season, we have the German military on furlough, and we have the Swiss. They come for the skiing and the climbing, only regulations don't allow visitors to go as high as before. We have some Italians too," she added.

24

"They tell me some of the guides are missing," Fenton said from the balcony.

And now the rustle of movement ceased behind her in the room. As suddenly as when she had spoken the name of Bastineau to the Frenchman in the train, the actual sound of silence fell upon the air.

"Ah, yes," said Madame Perrin after a moment. "Yes, there have been accidents," she said, and to Fenton it seemed that the Frenchman's same evasive and equivocal note was there.

"Accidents?" she asked, and now she stepped back into the room.

"Ah, yes," said Madame Perrin, and she sighed aloud as she moved from object to object, straightening this one and then that with her plump, pale, slightly dirty hand. "The same old story." She shrugged her shoulders. "Where do you expect the mountains to learn humanity from? Certainly not from men. Ropes break or rocks give away, and glaciers were never famous for their pity. There was a Swiss boy, a tourist he was, stopping at this hotel, who was killed with his guide in an avalanche last summer."

"Yes," said Fenton, "yes," and her eyes followed Madame Perrin. "Listen, *madame*," she said, and she closed her hands, cold and separate, in the pockets of her coat. "I came here for one thing," she said. "I want to know about Bastineau."

Again the familiar pause came, the seemingly interminable quiet in which the unseen, harking ear strained as if laid in the actual act of listening against the panel of a door. It was there for those who gave the answers as well as for those

25

who put the questions to the silence, and even as Madame Perrin spoke she seemed to listen in wariness.

"Ah, Bastineau," she said, and she moved the timepiece on the black marble mantel and flicked the dust away. "His people left, they closed the house and moved down into the valley." The shoulders in the black sweater shrugged again. "Most of their livestock was requisitioned, and then the question of soap came into it," she said. "His sisters couldn't make a living taking in washing with times what they are, and so with Bastineau gone there wasn't any reason to stay——"

"Gone?" said Fenton quickly.

"Down in the timber country they'd have vine leaves and wood ash for substitutes, anyway," Madame Perrin said, and for a moment her eyes almost met Fenton's. "Look at my hands!" she said. "I can't keep them clean any more! They haven't been clean for two years now. Look at the sheets on the bed! You can get along without coffee if you must, and you can get along without meat, and if you have to do without cigarettes, you do without them. But soap, oh, God in heaven, soap!" she said, and now she walked quickly to the balcony's doors and closed them fast against the morning air.

Fenton sat down on the side of the bed, her coat on still, and her eyes were fixed on Madame Perrin.

"What did you mean by Bastineau being gone? What did you mean by that?" she said.

Madame Perrin stopped before the desk, her hand moving as if to set the inkwell straight, and it was then that Fenton saw the little replica of Pétain standing by the blotting pad—the frail little manikin in khaki, not more than three inches

26

high. The fragile, ancient shoulders were stooped, and he was leaning on a cane, and under his kepi's visor his eyebrows were white and his cheeks as pink as a rose.

"What did Jacqueminot tell you about him?" Madame Perrin was saying, and her voice was suddenly low. She looked at Fenton now, the grotesque little puppet of France's surrender standing by her hand. "Jacqueminot—the guide who brought you here. What did he tell you about Bastineau?"

"That he was 'missing,'" said Fenton quickly.

"Yes, 'missing,'" said Madame Perrin, "'missing,' that is it."

"Only that isn't any answer," Fenton said in the same quick voice, "and I want the answer. In the meantime, you can take that gentleman out," she said, and she motioned toward the little man in khaki.

"One has to make the gesture. The tourists who come now like to see him here," said Madame Perrin, and she picked the Maréchal up by his feet and held him, head downward, in one hand.

"He's for sale—by the dozens—in the city," Fenton said. "For sale, like any object." She sat there, wearily, on the side of the bed. "Do you think I could have a piece of synthetic bread and something resembling coffee?" she said.

Madame Perrin made the eternal, national gesture, rubbing her thumb and forefinger together, with her eyebrows raised in query, and Fenton slipped the long strap of the navy suède bag from her shoulder, and opened it, and took the card out, and tore the ration tickets carefully away. And then Madame

27

Perrin went out the door, the ration tickets in her pocket, the figure of Pétain carried, head downward, in her hand.

It was late when Fenton awoke. The light had faded from the mountains, and the air from them was as cold as death, and she knew at once, with a new sense of hope in her heart, what there remained to do. She washed quickly in the water that ran icy from the tap, and she dressed again, and put a little of the coral lip rouge on her mouth, and combed out the longish, light hair. Downstairs, as she crossed through the hotel café to the village street, she saw a single client seated there, a man sitting alone, with his glass before him and a newspaper in his hands.

"I see you're off at once, like a good American, to save this corner of the world from rack and ruin," he called out in English to her, and she saw it was the Swiss who had looked up from his paper, his coat around his shoulders still as he had worn it in the train. On the table top, a packet of foreign-made cigarettes lay lavishly open, as not even the rich had them to leave open in times as bitter as these. "Sit down and have a very much watered Campari with me," he said.

Fenton had halted by the door, her hands deep in the pockets of her coat, her handbag slung by its strap from her shoulder, her silk stockings tapering to the buckles of her short-tongued, dark blue, military-looking shoes.

"I want to have a look around before the light is gone," she said. She faced him over the bare, bleak tables: the sleek, smooth, well-brushed head, the round, polished forehead, the full, freshly shaven jaws above the velvet collar of the city

28

coat. He looked exactly what he was, she thought: the wary businessman, the careful bourgeois, with—by some incongruity—a dueling scar drawing the left side of the mouth and puckering the cheek.

"I suppose there's no objection to my going along?" he said, and he came through the rows of tables to her. "I've had a discouraging time since I arrived. The business I came on is going to keep me here longer than I thought." He stopped before her, a tall, heavy, compactly built man. "My name is de Vaudois," he said, his light, sharp eyes upon her.

"Mine is Ravel," Fenton said.

"I'm a bit out of place here," he said as they went through the café door and into the village street together. "I've done some mountaineering in my time, but I wouldn't call it a natural bent. I'm not prepared for it," he said, and he kept step beside her as they turned toward the open square. "City suit, city shoes. I can't even find out where the avalanche came down or what guides can get me to it. I'm afraid I'll have to mix with people, inquire around a bit, before I can get anything accomplished. Not being American," he added with a touch of humor, "I find I'm not particularly interested in humanity."

"You should look up the mayor and the gendarmes and tell them why you're here," said Fenton, and de Vaudois made a gesture of impatience.

"I went to the mayor as a matter of course," he said. "He happens to be away for a fortnight. The chief of the *gendarmerie* is inclined to be difficult. It didn't occur to me that I'd need a permit to climb these mountains. But exactly who

29

has the authority to issue the permit, no one seems to know."

They were in the square now, where the monument stood, with the glaciers tipped white and perilous above them and the darkening land. Fenton walked directly to it in the failing light: to the figure of the mountaineer, tall, strong, and young, and done in bronze, who stood twice the size of a living man above the roll call of the dead. The statue's hand was raised to shade his eyes as he gazed upward to the mountain heights, seeking in season and out, through fog or sun, blizzard or rain, and century after century, for the movement of men lost who he knew must still be there. Below him, on the monument's granite, were written the names of the men from Truex who had died in this war or the other: first, the long list of dead with the letters turning green from the years of weather, and then the freshly cut names of those who had died in the war that was not yet done.

"I can't stand heights," the Swiss was saying irritably behind her. "Yet, here I am, trying to get permission to scramble up them for the sake of an old school friend whose son I didn't know."

Fenton's eyes went swiftly down the list of names—down the first, long, weathered columns of them to the last few chiseled sharply at the end. "Etienne Duclos, Michel Durand," she read in silence. There were not many of these new ones, and she leaned forward to read in the gathering twilight the two that remained below. "Michel Sabrone, Giovanni Venetto," the flavor of them seeming to bring closer the high, snowbound frontier. And *His name is not there*, she said in silence. *The name of Bastineau has not been written down.*

30

"Come," she said in sudden elation to the Swiss. "We'll go to the place where the guides used to take a glass of wine before their supper. Perhaps some of them still come in as they used to, and you could find out from them what there is to do." They turned back toward the village street, and whatever de Vaudois was saying, she did not hear it because of the strong, sweet urge of hope within her, the inexplicable conviction that Bastineau must answer now if she turned toward the mountains and called his name aloud. "Guides can often give more information than officials or men in uniform can," she said, and they came past the familiar doorsteps, the steep, cobbled alleys, the shopwindows in which miniature ice axes with edelweiss blooming in metal on them, doll-sized mountain boots to be pinned as insignia on the breast, all the chamois-hoofed-and-tufted souvenirs of mountaineering were still on futile display. They had come to the bridge which arched across the torrent as it fled swiftly through the town, and Fenton looked quickly for the ancient timber doorway of the guides' café on the other side. "These men know the mountains," she said to the Swiss. "The officials only know the regulations."

"That," said de Vaudois, with a certain dryness in his tone, "is exactly what I am counting on."

The figure of a girl could be seen coming toward them, crossing the bridge from the other side in the evening's half-light. She walked quickly, the head lowered, and de Vaudois drew himself in against the parapet to let her pass. She was dressed plainly, as a peasant girl might have been, with a dark wool scarf thrown over her head, and she would have hurried

31

by them if Fenton had not suddenly called out her name.

"Jeanne-Marie Favret! It is Jeanne-Marie, isn't it?" she said, and the girl stopped short and turned to where she stood.

"Yes," she said, briefly. "Yes," in a quiet voice, and she said nothing more.

"This is Fenton—Fenton Ravel," the American girl said in young and vulnerable eagerness.

"Yes," said the French girl, but she came no nearer. "The stationmaster said he had seen you this morning. Jacqueminot told me he had traveled up with you." The voice was cool, composed, and the hand holding the scarf at her throat was as pale as ivory in the dusk. "You've been gone some time. Three years," she said, and it may have been there that the rebuke lay, thought Fenton, for this was never the voice of friend speaking out in welcome to friend.

"This is Mademoiselle Favret, the mayor's daughter," Fenton said. Beneath them the waters rushed away from the fountainhead of still unfrozen springs and snows, and she said above its tumult: "This is Monsieur de Vaudois."

"Yes," said the French girl quietly. "I know."

And *Why does she stand at a distance from me now,* thought Fenton; *why is she silent with me as if we had never walked these streets arm in arm together, and never kissed each other's cheeks as sisters, never danced on the Fourteenth of July in the streets together, never skied down the trails at Christmas with torches in our hands?*

"I've been trying to find your father all afternoon," de Vaudois said, and then he burst out in irritation: "Why the devil does a village have a mayor if you can't get within speaking distance of him?"

"My father is away," said Jeanne-Marie, and Fenton seemed to hear as well the passion of another answer that was not said aloud.

"I came here intending to spend twenty-four hours," de Vaudois said, and he pulled his overcoat around his shoulders impatiently. "And now I find I'm expected to cool my heels like any mountain native until the mayor chooses to come back!"

"The natives of Truex are men of courage," the French girl said. She stood tense and motionless on the bridge before them, her features indiscernible in the growing dark, even the startling white of her hand on the scarf now going dim.

"I've sat up all night in a third-class carriage," said de Vaudois testily, "and I've met with nothing but disorganization and lack of authority here. Why the mayor of a town can't leave explicit orders when he goes off——"

"Men under arrest are not permitted to give orders," the French girl said quietly.

"Under arrest?" repeated Fenton, speaking scarcely aloud.

The strong, cold avalanche of mountain water poured downward in the dark beneath the bridge, and now the first stars were suddenly there above them, single and clear and luminous as stars are at a height.

"Yes," said the French girl. "He was arrested yesterday."

"And the nature of his crime?" asked de Vaudois, clipping the words short.

The French girl did not move for a moment; she had

33

seemed even to have ceased to breathe across the little space of night.

"His crime was that he remained a Frenchman," she said, and the pride and pain of it were in her voice now. "It is the gravest crime one can commit today."

She had turned swiftly, and she would have gone from them, but Fenton called her name again across the sound of the cold, rushing, mountain tide.

"Jeanne-Marie, come back to the hotel with me!" she cried quickly and grievously to her. "There is so much for us to say!"

"What is there for me to say to you, Fenton, except that we do not want strangers in our country now?" the French girl said, halting and turning back. "You should know this, you who have French blood in your veins! You were here in the good years with us, and when war and the bad years came, you went away. And now we do not want curious, idle strangers coming back to mix with us. We do not want to be spied on in our grief!" she cried across the dark.

She was gone from them, moving quickly off across the bridge, the sound of her steps on the cobbles wiped out by the water's deep-throated roar. A street light shone dimly at the corner now, and Fenton watched her pass through its cone of illumination, hastening still, and disappear into the darkness of the twisting streets.

"You and I are rather *persona non grata* here," the Swiss said dryly.

"Come," said Fenton. "Let us get your business arranged

34

quickly," and she walked in wild, young bitterness before him to the doorway of the guides' café.

At its threshold, she pushed the familiar door open before he could raise his hand and touch it, and she stepped before him into the low-beamed room. For a moment she could see nothing in the barely lit obscurity, and she paused there, remembering the faces of the others who had sat there, fearless and young, and their voices calling from table to table, and the warble of a yodeler's song, or a mouth organ playing, and now there was nothing but silence here. And *The last time*, she thought, *the last time he was with me. We sat at that table, and he kissed me like the ring put on to wear forever, and outside the tocsin was ringing slowly and terribly the speechless sound of war.*

The dimness thinned and cleared now as she waited, and she saw that the tables were placed as they had been in other years—the strong, thick-limbed tables with benches set along them on either side, and the lamp with the green metal shade hung from the center beam as it had always hung. On the walls were the two framed pictures done in embroidery floss: the one of the wooden-faced French soldier in horizon blue tied to a stake with the Germans lashing at him; and the one, painstakingly done in French knots and feather stitching, of the full, bleeding heart on which the embroidered inscription ran, *A Frenchman's Heart in German Prison Camp, 1914–1918*. But except for three men sitting drinking at the farthest table in one corner's gloom, the place was empty and the benches were bare.

35

"*Salut*," said Fenton, looking toward them, and "*Salut*," their three voices answered her.

"Typically Latin, these places," de Vaudois said, speaking English now. "Picturesque but unsanitary." He followed her to the table, and settled himself in opposite her, with his back turned to the rest of the café. He took out his folded handkerchief and wiped off the table's timber before he placed his elbows on it, and then he looked at Fenton on the other side. "Collaboration or merely appeasement," he said, his clean, well-manicured fingers interlocked, and the elaborate wristwatch shining on his wrist, "I observe you accept conditions very well."

"For me," said Fenton, her young eyes gravely on him, "this is coming home."

Beyond him were the three men at the corner table, two with pipes in their mouths and their glasses of diluted drink before them, and the third with his back turned to them. They were mountain men, in ancient jackets, with weather-worn, felt hats on their heads, and their words were given and taken slowly, in the deliberate way of mountain men. In a moment, the old man came out through the kitchen door and crossed the café to the table, and Fenton watched him come. It might have been three years back, and the same workman's blue canvas apron knotted around his waist, and the sound on the flagstones made by the same manure-caked shoes. But the mustaches that hung long and stained across his mouth were whiter, and as he came to the table and laid his veined hand on it, she saw there was scarcely the look of sight left in his red-rimmed, corroded eyes.

36

"Monsieur Chatelard, how are you?" she said in a low voice to him, and the ancient hand with the cloth on it halted as he wiped the table's timber clean.

"As you see me, *mademoiselle*," he said slowly, and then this ghost risen from her childhood and from her girlhood leaned closer to search the features of her face. "You used to come here———" He was groping for it, fumbling uncertainly back across the years.

"I had my first grenadine here," she said to him. "You carved me a bird that whistled. When I did my first glacier —the Bossons, it was—I carried the stick that you made me, the one with the serpent wound around it with the apple in his mouth."

As she talked, the old man's eyes cleared, and a spark of what might have been hope, or sight, or life itself redeemed showed milkily between the lids.

"You are Mademoiselle Ravel," he said slowly, and he put his hand out, and his fingers touched her hair.

"We would like to order," said de Vaudois, laying his coat aside. "What have you got that's drinkable?"

But the old man did not seem to hear him speak. The square, ancient hands, that were neither clean nor dirty but simply scarred with time and use, were spread on the table for support while the face was turned, incredulous still, toward Fenton.

"Yes," he said, his voice peaceful now as he spoke. "You were gone a long time. Did you hear what happened? Did you hear the Boches came back while you were away?"

37

"Yes," said Fenton, and she laid her hand on his. "They told us."

"Did they tell you they took two million of our men?" he said, his voice rising a little. "Took them prisoner, and killed another hundred thousand?" he said.

"Yes," said Fenton. "They told us. They told us that, too."

"I remember the last days you came," he said, and his fingers touched her hair again. "You came here with Bastineau."

Had the name been the crack of gunfire across the room, the third man at the corner table could not have sprung more quickly to life. He swung his legs over the bench on which he sat and brought his feet down hard upon the flaggings. Then he stood up, with the scraping of hobnailed boots on stone. He was dressed as the others were, in a short climbing jacket and knickerbockers, and a brimmed, shapeless hat with medals on it was on his head, and a pipe was bitten between his teeth.

"*Bon soir, m'sieu', 'dame,*" he said, and Fenton saw it was the Frenchman of the train.

"*Bon soir,*" said de Vaudois, and he turned in his seat. "Come over here and help me out. I don't know what to order in a place like this, *monsieur—monsieur——*"

"Jacqueminot's the name," the Frenchman said.

He lifted one leg and then the other over the bench on which de Vaudois sat, and he seated himself beside him, his pipe between his teeth still, his eyes on Fenton's face.

"I'll have cognac and water, Monsieur Chatelard," she said.

38

"I can taste it already," said de Vaudois, his mouth twisting sideways in distaste. "Foul and impotent and slightly warm. Bring me some of that monstrous *gin national*," he said, and the old man moved away.

"Monsieur Chatelard made the needlework pictures on the wall," said Fenton to the Swiss. "It wasn't any woman's hand. He did them himself, after the last war, when he came home from prison camp in Germany. That's himself, with the Germans lashing him. And the other one is of his own heart, which the Germans couldn't see."

"Decorative," said de Vaudois, and then he turned to Jacqueminot. "I can't get anywhere with the authorities here," he said. "I find the mayor of the place under arrest, and the *gendarmerie* of no help at all. At least one is spared this absolute disorganization in the Occupied Zone."

"In the event that one's life and liberty are spared as well," said Jacqueminot.

"Now, this is a military zone," de Vaudois said, and as he made his points he checked them on his fingers, one by one. "The terms of Italy's armistice with France declared it so. But France was conquered by the Germans—am I right? While at the same time, the French are nominally in authority. Now, which official of what nationality should have the power to issue me a permit allowing me to climb a mountain and remove a Swiss boy's body from under several tons of snow?"

"We'll take it up with the *chef de brigade*," Jacqueminot said, and Fenton watched the quick, sharp, elfin profile of his face. The old man had returned with the bottles and glasses,

39

carrying them carefully on his little tray. As he placed them on the table, feeling his way to set each of them down, Jacqueminot touched his shoulder. "Bring me a *café national, gran'père,*" he said. "I'd like it hot. I have a long way to go."

"You are going off again tonight?" said Fenton, and she felt the sense of bereavement again, as if his going took away what might be revealed of Bastineau.

"Yes," said Jacqueminot, and his eyes met hers in what may have been accusation, or what may have been merely conjecture as to why she had brought de Vaudois here. "No more importation allowed under the genial regime in which we live for the moment," he said. "So I pack a rucksack full of wool— when I have the luck to get it—and carry it up the mountain to the peasant women. They copy the Norwegian patterns for me, and work it into mittens for the skiing trade."

The old man came back across the café room and put the cup of steaming liquid down on the table before the Frenchman.

"You carry it up at night?" said de Vaudois. He spoke with a certain irony, and then he took a taste of the gin and apparently found it unpleasant on his tongue. "And after a night like last night, spent sitting in the train! What energy the French race has in spite of all we hear about its disintegration!"

For a moment the thing lit savagely in Jacqueminot's eyes, and then he turned to the cup of coffee at his place.

"In periods of slow starvation, the stomach is the timepiece and the calendar," he said. "There is no night and day." He lifted the lead spoon from the saucer and studied the tablet of saccharine that lay, small as a pinhead, in it, before he tipped it into the liquid in his cup. "During the hours of light, there's the land to work," he said. "It's poor and rocky enough here, but we need everything it can give." Fenton saw the lines that were striped across his forehead, and the deeper gashes that marked his cheeks, and she thought: *He is a young man, but his face is young no longer. Out of some kind of protest I do not know the name of yet, he has given his youth away.* "In times like these," he was saying, "men do not exchange their native soil for what seems a better one, unless they are driven to it. So I am staying here and working mine." He watched the saccharine pill drop like a parachutist into his cup of *café national* and, spinning, open its floating, white umbrella of infinitesimal foam. "I am trying to clean the stones and weeds and other foreign matter from the soil," he said, giving the bitterness of his voice to them to interpret as they would.

There was silence at the table as Jacqueminot turned the spoon slowly in his cup, and de Vaudois made a wry face, drinking the watered gin.

"Where do they get the labels for this stuff?" he suddenly broke out. "Genuine English labels to all appearances, and this putrefaction inside." He set his glass down in annoyance. "Like the anti-Vichy propaganda that is prevalent. Paid for in English cash, and served at any café table by the unemployed French who aren't particular how they pick up a hundred francs or so."

Fenton saw that the color had gone from under the sunburn of Jacqueminot's face, and then he put the pipe savagely back between his teeth, and felt in his pocket for the substance that no one called tobacco any more. As he filled his pipe bowl with it with a steady hand, he looked in unmistakable accusation at her.

"You asked me about a friend of yours this morning, a guide you used to know," he said, and he sucked the pipe's smoke in. "I don't know whether Madame Perrin, or Jeanne-Marie, or any other of your old friends has told you since——"

"Told me what?" said Fenton as his voice paused. She felt her lips moving stiffly on the words. "Told me what?" she said.

So he gave the story to her, telling it across the table to her, scarcely aware, it seemed, that the room was quiet, listening, or that the Swiss was there. The guides had been mobilized on the frontier outposts all during the winter of France's war, he said. Once or twice in the spring there had been a little skirmish with the Italians, enough to keep them all on the alert, and that was all they saw. And then, in June, the laying down of arms had come. Pétain had asked the Germans for armistice terms, and the men stationed in the high mountain posts knowing as little as any other Frenchmen how or why.

"You were there, too?" asked Fenton in a quick, low voice.

"Yes, I was there," said Jacqueminot, and she did not speak again but drank the watered cognac quickly and jerkily down.

In the week following the surrender, Jacqueminot went on, Bastineau and two others of the garrison set out on a reconnaissance tour. Hostilities were not suspended yet, and they went on military duty, he said. They were all on skis, they were roped together, and they wore their *chasseurs alpins* uniform.

42

"It was the dark blue of that uniform that showed us the depth at which they lay," said Jacqueminot, with no compromise remaining in his voice. "A snow bridge had broken under them. We found the three of them in the crevasse. Bastineau had been leading," he said. "During the maneuvers to get the bodies out, the rope that held him severed through, and he fell deeper into the schrund." He looked across the table at her, the dark eyes hopelessly beyond compassion now. "I had hoped you would hear it from Madame Perrin—from anyone but me," he said.

De Vaudois turned on the bench and called out toward the kitchen for another glass of gin.

"I heard the story myself this afternoon," he said, turning back. "The chemist told me about it when we talked of mountain accidents. A satisfactory way, I should think," he said pleasantly, "for a mountaineer to die."

And now it was finished. The thing was said and done, and Jacqueminot got to his feet, and stood there a moment looking down at Fenton, who sat motionless at the table still, her eyes stricken, her face incredibly pale, the mute mouth tremulous and young.

"*Bon soir*," said Jacqueminot quietly, and, as if in some spirit of contrition, he held out his hand.

Fenton was standing now, her fingers fumbling the coat closed, seeking the buttons blindly and not finding them there.

"It was better hearing it from you," she said. "It was better like this," and then she turned quickly and went out the door.

Outside the night had grown tall and powerful, like an actual presence in the street. The vast waters rushed on be-

43

neath the bridge, the tall, speechless mountains rose, and Fenton's blood trembled in her as she took the direction of the hotel on the station square. She walked fast, her head down, her hands in the pockets of her coat, walking blindly from street light to shadow, with the solitary sound of her own hastening steps ringing aloud in the narrow streets. As she turned the corner, she heard de Vaudois' voice behind her, calling out her name. And *Cannot I have even this in silence,* she thought in desperation as she hurried on. She was almost at the hotel door when de Vaudois caught her up, and then the firm, imperious hand closed on her shoulder in the dark.

"For an American, you are strangely unmethodical," he said, and he swung her around toward him. "Listen to me," he said, his voice savage as it had never been before. "We are being asked to get out of Truex, you and I," he said. "It is being requested of us in several different ways. I have work to do here. I have no intention of getting out." His hand was firm on her shoulder still, and she felt his breath upon her face. "And if you have the spirit I think you have," he said, "you won't go either—not until you've found out what it is they're trying to do. We're foreigners among them, you and I, and we're not wanted here."

As he paused for an instant, Fenton drew back from him and shook her head in protest.

"No, no, they're my people!" she cried out, but she heard the helpless sound of it, lost like a child's cry in the mountains' vast, impersonal dark.

"There are any number of interesting facts to be found in the church records here," de Vaudois went on saying. He

44

dropped his hand from her shoulder, and took his cigarette case from his pocket, and then he struck a light. "Will you have one?" he said. Fenton stood on the hotel step above him now, and, as if in refusing the cigarette she refused the actual terms of whatever armistice he offered, she shook her head again. "I don't know, of course," said de Vaudois, holding the match to his, "just how much of the Notre-Dame Chapel we can accept as the original—seventeenth century, I believe it was—but you should plan to spend some time at least studying the ecclesiastical archives there. Now, take the story of the three dead guides," he said. "Not being able to get on with that business of my own, I glanced over the death register, and the record of Masses sung and military funerals held." The dark was suddenly quick with it now, with the actual shape of harking, the whole country, it might have been, listening for the sound of what would come. "For instance, there has not been a funeral service read for three *chasseurs alpins* in Truex—only for two. Their names are to be found inscribed on the monument to the dead we visited this evening." De Vaudois pronounced the words slowly and exactly as he smoked his cigarette below her in the village street. "And another curiosity," he added, "if Bastineau is dead, there has never—in this devout community!—been a Mass said for the repose of the poor devil's soul."

Two

THE NEXT day was a fair one, but the peasants who had come down from the mountains, with their milk tins strapped to their backs, were saying that the weather would not hold. It would break tomorrow or the next day, they said as Fenton crossed the square among them, and she looked up at the delicate cloud that hung like a halo over Mont Blanc's icy brow. She was dressed for the place now, in the gray, corduroy knickerbockers and the heavy, nailed boots of climbing countries, with a blue scarf knotted at her neck, and a short jacket buttoned tight from throat to hip. Her hair was pale as wheat

46

in the morning light, and she had put no rouge on her mouth, and her eyes were water clear beneath her smooth, dark brows. She would climb to the chalet that was home, she thought; for the first time in three years, she would put the key in the lock of its door, and open its windows to the sun. But as she passed among the dark-garbed, single-syllabled peasants, she saw among them those she knew.

There was Marc, whose mind was that of a child, and whose eyes were the color of heaven; and Dizot, who set bones in place with the canny touch of his hands. And Virgil was there, with the hump on his back, and she knew the lift of his hunch-back's chin, and the proud, defiant look in his eye. Every summer he had fallen drunk into the stream, and his voice had been heard through the chalet windows as he lay all night in the water's bed and talked softly to the stars. But because of Jeanne-Marie's words of the night before, Fenton hastened past them. *We do not want strangers in our country now*, she could hear the French girl saying. And *They will not have to say it again to me*, thought Fenton, and she looked ahead at the mountains. *If I do not look into their faces, they need not tell me that I am not wanted here.*

But it was *monsieur le curé* himself who stopped her by the water trough, the ascetic face gone thinner, the lines etched closer on it, but the alert eyes unaltered beneath the hat's curved brim.

"So you have come," he said quietly as he held her hand, and it might have been a question that he put her. "The ship founders, and rats flee, but the gulls come back to the mast with their wings spread——"

47

"Yes," said Fenton. "I am perhaps useless, but I have come."

"Ah, well, things are changed! Asthma keeps me from climbing as I did," said *monsieur le curé*, and he rapped his chest with one lean, aging hand. "But my hearing is good still —excellent—and my memory astonishes me at times." The skin was drawn tight across the nose's sharp, veined arch and the high blades of the cheekbones. The thin lips, wrinkled like silk, were smiling as if at the mysteries of age. "Dates in history—1789, for instance. Other years in which Frenchmen were hungry." She saw that the black skirts of his frock were rusty, and the leather of his shoes was cut deep across from wear. "I recite whole chapters to them from the pulpit now," he said, and he looked up at the mountains and smiled the quiet, enigmatic smile. "Many men of my age—nearly seventy—carry ear trumpets into which certain dosages of truth and information are poured," he said, "but my hearing is my solace. I can hear Boston, on clear nights, as well as if Massachusetts were no farther than the transept——"

And now it was Cousin Perrin who joined them, and who stopped, planted solid as rock before Fenton, and held out his hand.

"*B'en*, this weather is like the armistice we're having—it can't last," he said, and the other peasants standing near by in the square opened their blunt-toothed mouths and roared aloud. Cousin Perrin was the village's pride of wit and decision—a man of fifty or more, with a strong, lean jaw and shoulders like a timber yoke, and whichever way the wind was blowing, the truth of it was spoken in his mouth. "The signs

48

of it are there if you get so you can read them," he said, and his bright, dark, stubborn eyes looked from under the black felt brim at Fenton and the curé. "Weather's always temporary—any kind—good or bad. It's like crops and the berry season. Provided you've lived long enough, you'll know when the break is due." His mustaches hung long and dark across his mouth, and he gave no hint of smiling. He had not smiled, Fenton remembered it was said of him, and he had not spoken to his sister-in-law and his brother in the village since the quarrel about the goat in 1932. "Time you came back," he said in his slow, heavy, mountain speech to Fenton. "In time to see us carrying our milk down like a herd of pack mules for them," and he turned aside and spat upon the ground.

The one called Marc came close to them then, his blue eyes moving, wide and blank, on Fenton's face.

"We can't walk into a *bistro* and have a glass of wine before starting up the mountain!" he said incredulously to her. "They've taken even the wine away!"

"Wine!" admonished the curé now, and his voice and his eyes were quick with rebuke. "Wine you can do without. Speak of worthier things to those who come back among us!"

The humpback joined the group by the water trough, and as he shook Fenton's hand as the others had done, in his face there was neither welcome nor wonder, but merely acceptance that she was there.

"*Mademoiselle*, with a glass of wine on the table, the mind worked faster," he said, his voice pitched tense and high. "Once we'd sit down at the *bistro* table before going up the mountain, and when thoughts came to us, we'd speak them

49

out! We didn't stand like cattle in the square like this, hanging our heads——"

"*B'en*, if you need a glass of wine to make a patriot and an honorable man of you, then you'd better go back and sleep in the stream as you did in other years!" Cousin Perrin cried out, and at the sound of it, the black-clad others guffawed aloud.

"Virgil," said the curé then, "have you heard what General de Pâques did when he came upon Frenchmen roistering in the days of the defeat? The General had lost his right arm at Verdun, over twenty years ago," he said, "and he had a hook in the place of it. During the 1940 retreat, he passed through a village where soldiers were drinking and making merry, and he rushed in like a fury among them and struck their faces with his hook of an arm, and slashed their uniforms across. 'This is a time of national disaster!' he shouted at them. 'Then grieve like men of courage!' "

The curé's voice had rung aloud across the square, and now that he ceased speaking, the peasants stood silent a moment as they might have stood in their pews at church when the sermon was done. Before he moved off through the groups of them, he lifted one hand as if in benediction, and then he crossed the square, an erect, frail figure walking without haste toward the village street, with the shabby skirts of his cassock swinging at his heels.

"Come," said Cousin Perrin, turning to Fenton. "Come up to the farm and say *bon jour* to La Cousine."

Fenton's heart went warm and quick with joy as she walked up the road, side by side with Cousin Perrin. *The peasants*

have not turned from me, she thought. *Whatever Jeanne-
Marie and Jacqueminot fear in me, the peasants have not
turned away. There'll be La Cousine, and the sons, and we'll
sit in the kitchen and talk as we did in the years before.* Inside
her jacket she carried the little package, done in tissue paper
and tied with gilded string—a pair of kid gloves and two lace
handkerchiefs from New York for Cousin Perrin's wife, because year after year, season on season, they had talked in the
high pasture fields or in the farm kitchen together, woman
and girl, until the war had come.

"The new heifers didn't calve this spring," Cousin Perrin
was saying as they went up the road together. His black hat
was set low on his brows, and the side of his weathered face
was grim, and house by house the village dropped behind
them as they climbed. It was said of him too, thought Fenton,
that no one but Cousin Perrin's wife and his confessor had
ever seen him without his hat, and she knew she had laughed
out loud the first time she had heard it. *I was standing with
Bastineau on the post-office steps, and the snow was falling,
and the flakes of it melted fast on the back of his glove.* "The
heifers didn't calve because they knew what would come of it
if they did," Cousin Perrin was saying. "You come back to
France in the year that the signs are being given." He spoke
sternly as an oracle to her, with the milk tin rattling empty on
his back. "Take the hens. They're on to the occupation. They
lay eggs the size of walnuts now, or else they've stopped laying altogether. They know as well as we do that eggs aren't
laid for Frenchmen any more."

"Do you see *them* here, sitting drinking in the cafés, as we do in Lyon?" Fenton said, the pronoun designating that special race whose name they did not speak. "Do you see them walking through the streets, with the gendarmes saluting them as if they were superior officers? Do you have the humility of that here? In Lyon, the French call them 'The Parisians.' I like that, somehow," she said. "I laugh out loud every time I hear it, because whatever they've done, it means they haven't been able to take that kind of wit away."

"We do not see them here in uniform," said Cousin Perrin, and he looked ahead at the mountains, and past them, as if at the actual flesh and features of defeat. "But we know the look of them well enough. They requisition the cows for slaughter, they order the fodder pitched out of the lofts, and the pigs driven forth from the sties. They've sown secret agents like corn through the hills—one here, one there—to spy upon us. And today we learn that they've taken our mayor away."

"How high am I allowed to climb with you?" asked Fenton.

To the right now lay the pathway to the chalet, and she halted on the wagon road and looked for the sight of its roof through the trees.

"There's no law worth respecting," said Cousin Perrin, his voice irate and strong, "that would keep any man or woman of good will from walking through the hills. Your chalet," he said, and he stopped beside her. "It's stood there empty since the day you left. No lights in the windows at night, no smoke in the chimney—it was a sad thing to walk past it for us who knew the family well. Three years without human breath being drawn in it. Have you come back without your people?" he said.

"I came back alone to work," said Fenton. "We've brought food with us. We've been distributing it."

"Food?" he said, and his voice was suddenly sharp. They were walking again, climbing by the mountain torrent, and the way was steep, and their nailed shoes slid upon the stones. "You have food with you?"

"In Lyon," said Fenton. "We feed babies and school children and students there."

The Calvary stood ahead, the wooden arms of it spread as if in supplication to the high snow mountains and the impervious sky. *And here the way forks*, she remembered; *to the left you climb to the higher habitations, and to the right the pathway to the glaciers lies.* They kept to the left, Cousin Perrin climbing ahead, and entered the waterfall's area of sound. The Calvary was close now, the wood of it gray from the years of weather, the step that lay beneath it polished and worn from the knees that had bent there in prayer. Cousin Perrin made the sign of the cross before it, and then he too kneeled down as the others had done through the years, and Fenton waited. In the moment that he kneeled there, she saw the look of endurance in his face, and her heart smote her with pain.

"Cousin Perrin, I have not asked you about your sons," she said, when he had risen to his feet, and the sound of her voice was carried from them, down the water's roaring fall. But Cousin Perrin heard the words, and still his straight back did not falter as he led the way ahead.

"Prisoners," he said grimly. "Both of them prisoners. They

53

set the prisoners to work on the land over there, the newspapers tell us. Frenchmen—nearly two million of them—walking behind a foreigner's plow, tilling a foreigner's soil," he said, and his voice was strong in castigation, and his back as straight as timber as he climbed. "La Cousine and I, we do the work here together, as we did before the boys were grown——"

They came to the sight of the farmhouse now, set high in a clearing of the pines. The space of mud before it was frozen hard as stone and patterned with footmarks; those of the cows stamped in heavy, icy bracelets from the doorway to the wooden trough where the spring water quivered cold and deep, and the prints of the goats laid neat and small, like fossil marks of shells in the stony soil. They passed the pigsty, which was built against the house itself, and the single, great, soiled beast came out, the folds of her neck hanging slack, and she eyed them craftily between the boards.

"One left," said Cousin Perrin, the sound of it bitter. "When she is covered and litters in the spring, they'll take the young away."

He slipped the milk tin off his shoulders at the door, and he stood it upright against the stone of the step, and Fenton followed him in past the chickens which stalked, lean and wary-eyed, in and out of the open door. In the cold, stone entranceway, the Virgin stood in her niche still, the straw flowers in the tumbler before her blooming yellow and blue and scarlet as they had always bloomed. The smell of cattle was strong here in the house, and the sound of their voices, moaning a little, could be heard beyond the wall.

"Nothing has changed," said Fenton, and she followed him in cold, strange elation toward the dark shape of the heavy kitchen door.

"Things have been like this too long to change," said Cousin Perrin. "We've had landslides and torrents every spring that carried half the mountain past us. We've had avalanches in winter that bore the trees in the forest down like kindling to our door. But the house has stood winter and spring and summer like this for a century and a quarter. It's not the happenings of three years that can cause it to change." He felt for the latch of the kitchen door in the stone wall's dark, and at the sound of his hand on it the two dogs on the other side started barking aloud. They were playing the same foolish scene now that they had always played, thought Fenton, but once in the kitchen with her hand laid on the brow of one and then the other of them, she saw that their muzzles were white now and they had not been before. "Down, cretins!" cried Cousin Perrin to them, and the dogs crept back behind the fire again, their collielike, bastard heads lowered, their tails trailed in apology as they drew them in between their legs. "Madeleine!" said Cousin Perrin, speaking his wife's name to the room's obscurity. "A friend come back from America is here!"

What light there was in the room came through the chimney's opening in the roof, and through the two small windows in the eastern wall. Tin cans that held geranium stubs were set on the tipped wooden window sills, and the pages of almanacs and calendars from other years were pinned fading to the smoke-stained timber. The tall, grim woman seated at

55

the table stood up in the corner's dark, her gray blouse buttoned to her lean neck, her hair drawn tightly back, and she laid her knitting down.

"If you bring friends, they're welcome to come in and sit with us," La Cousine Perrin said. "But the others who come to take their pick of the stock, you can leave them at the door!"

Fenton crossed the room quickly to her, and took her hand, but the Frenchwoman gave no sign. She stood there, looking into Fenton's eyes, but not as if into vehicles of sight or of communication, but as if into windows that opened upon some scene or vision that she alone could see. Fenton took the little package from her jacket, and spoke almost shyly to her.

"I brought you a pair of gloves to wear to Mass," she said, "and a lace handkerchief to carry," but La Cousine shook her head.

"A handkerchief to wipe my tears!" she said steadily to Fenton, and even now she did not seem to look into Fenton's face, but past it through the same bitterly revealing window's glass. What it was she looked upon could not be said—perhaps the field of a foreign country, with the figure of a Frenchman in it, bent to a plow that was not his; perhaps the slope of a mountainside, like the one they had just mounted, with a footpath winding through the trees, and two tall young men hurrying up it, taking the short cut home. "Do you think I've sat here crying for my sons?" she said to Fenton. "Not as long as there were better things to do for them, better than shedding tears!"

The moaning and stamping of the cattle could be heard beyond the wall, and with his hat on still Cousin Perrin walked to the fire that smoldered, not in a chimneyplace but on a flat broad slab of stone at one side of the room, and he stooped and laid a dry, thick fan of brush across it. An iron arm set in the wall held the caldron out above the smoking ash, and he pushed it aside on its hinge as he squatted there. Between the wall and the hearthstone, the two dogs were stretched as if in death, their long coats matted, the tough, broken cushions of their paws turned to the fire's head. Above Cousin Perrin's head, the Savoyard chimney stood open like a doorway high above—as tall as a mine shaft and made of timber, with the thread of smoke that rose now from the fire on the kitchen floor drawn upright through the room and into its square, charred avenue. Here in the beamed ceiling it opened square and wide to the room below, broad enough for six men, walking abreast, to have passed through it. But at its top it tapered so steeply that the body of only one man could have passed through and dropped outside to the wooden shingles of the roof.

"Madeleine," said Cousin Perrin from where he stooped by the fire, "they took the mayor off yesterday."

"The mayor!" said La Cousine. "Jean-Pierre Favret! He married us. God in heaven," she said, scarcely aloud. "They're going one by one!"

And *One by one, one by one*, repeated Fenton's heart in silence, *one by one they go. Bastineau once sat at this table and ate bread and cheese with us, and now he is here no longer. The country was rich then, and there were hams strung up to smoke in the chimney shaft, and Bastineau sang the song of the mountain infantry, he sang "L'Infant'rie Al-*

57

pine, voilà mes amours" as wild and stirring as bugles playing in the room. And Bastineau sprang light as a cat to pull
the trap door in the chimney closed, because the snow was
driving down the shaft and hissing on the flame. Perrin's sons
were pitching the straw from the cattle room out steaming on
the drifts, and La Cousine sat at this table with us, laughing
like a girl.

"One by one they've gone from us," said Cousin Perrin
from the fire. "We've lost Socquet, Ravanel, Couttet; we've
lost Durand, Sabrone—and we've lost Bastineau." He said
the name without warning, and Fenton felt the blood ebb
swiftly from her heart. "And now Favret," he said. "They've
taken Favret away!"

"What will they do to him?" said Fenton, and her lips
moved stiffly on the words.

"Socquet and Couttet went like that," said Cousin Perrin
from where he stooped by the fire. "They knocked on their
doors one night, and we never heard of them after that. Ravanel set up the mountain toward Les Mouilles with a pack
on his back one day at dawn, and we never heard of him after.
Durand and Sabrone were brought down dead—killed on the
glacier. We got their bodies out of the crevasse, but whether
it was accident or not——" He shrugged his shoulders.

"And Bastineau?" said Fenton, and her tongue was dry in
her mouth. "What of Bastineau?"

"The secret police have been up three times, putting questions to us," La Cousine said in bitterness, and she looked
again at the vision through the unseen pane of glass. "They'll
pay as high as the family for proof that he didn't die."

"Because of him, they took Favret off," said Cousin Perrin from the fire. "They questioned him all the night before about Bastineau. Favret gave them his oath that he was dead. Jeanne-Marie heard him through the door."

"But if Bastineau is dead," said Fenton, and she heard the desperate sound of her own voice asking it of them now. "If he is dead, why has Mass for him never been said?"

"The Church cannot take the word of man," said Cousin Perrin. He looked at Fenton. "What do you know of the Swiss who has come to Truex?" he said.

"We came on the train together," said Fenton. "He has come to find the body of a dead friend who was killed in August by the snow."

"A friend!" said Cousin Perrin in contempt.

"I did not see him this morning in the village," Fenton said.

"He was behind us," said Cousin Perrin, squatting by the fire. "He was close enough to touch you, when we stood talking with the others in the square."

La Cousine's strong, work-worn hand dropped suddenly on Fenton's arm now, and her mouth was grim.

"Why are you back? Why are you here?" she said, and she looked no longer at the vision of another place or time, but in doubt at the shape of miscreance that might be standing before them.

"She has come back with food," said Cousin Perrin, and he got up from the fire and pushed the iron arm that held the caldron in place again above the flame. "She is feeding the hungry in Lyon," he said. "She is serving as well."

La Cousine's fingers pressed fiercer now on Fenton's arm,

59

and she drew her to the table. There on the clean, unpainted timber of it was the knitting she had laid down—the ball of cream, and the ball of black, and the four steel needles shaping the mitten out. Fenton saw the Norwegian pattern of it partially done: the strong-toothed edge, and the arrows, and the antlers, and the symbols of Nordic fortitude.

"You will knit for us," said La Cousine, and her voice was low and eager. Her eyes had relinquished the other sight that held them fast, and they searched the features of Fenton's face. "I have six pairs to finish by tomorrow night. The cheese-making has held me back. If you will do a pair, the lot will be done."

"I can knit simple things," said Fenton in hesitation.

"But you follow a pattern," La Cousine said sharply to her, and the fingers closed hard again on Fenton's arm. "You follow it stitch by stitch," she said. "You'll do this for us. I'll give you the wool to work with, and the pattern. You'll follow it exactly. You will not make a mistake because a mistake can mean the loss of men," she said.

Cousin Perrin crossed the room to where the two women sat at the table, and he hung his black jacket up with care on the hook on the cheese-room door.

"She knits all day," he said, looking down at them. "It makes the time pass for her."

"Time pass!" La Cousine cried bitterly. "Every stitch I make is a tear that doesn't run down my face!" The needles were in her fingers now, and she leaned toward Fenton. "Watch! It goes like this," she said, and she worked the wool

60

slowly so that the girl might see. "You'll take the wool down with you. You'll finish a pair by tomorrow night. I do not ask this idly of you. Do not accept it idly," she said.

"But, La Cousine," said Fenton, speaking gently to her, "the skiing season hasn't begun. Why must you hurry?" She looked at the sharp, set features of the woman's face, and she thought: *Grief has done this to her. It has put that look of another time and place in her eyes. It has twisted the thoughts in her head, and taken all logic from her.* "There are no skiers in Truex yet, La Cousine," Fenton said.

"Skiers!" cried out La Cousine in contempt, and she blended the black wool savagely with the white, and drew the stitches through. "I do them for my own sons, and for the sons of other women!"

"You mean—you send them? You can get them across the frontier?" asked Fenton. Cousin Perrin had sat down at the table with them in his shirt sleeves and suspenders, and he looked gravely at her from under his hat's brim across the table's boards.

"We get them over the frontier," said La Cousine, and the needles moved swiftly in the wool.

"My woman speaks the truth," said Cousin Perrin in his deep, slow speech. "We get them across the frontier."

"But how?" asked Fenton.

"How," said Cousin Perrin, "we do not ask."

"If you have come back to serve, then serve!" said La Cousine, and the needles clicked, and the ash broke quietly on the hearth.

61

There was nothing more said until Cousin Perrin took the mimeographed single sheet of paper from the table's drawer and laid it before Fenton.

"Things take place which we are not intended to hear of," he said. "And yet no power on earth can keep us from hearing of them. This paper does not come to us often, and it comes with difficulty, but when we have it, then we know we are not alone. We learn the truth from it," he said, and the blunt black nail of his forefinger followed the unevenly inked words across the page. "Here it is that Herriot has returned his Legion of Honor to Vichy," said the slow, heavy, mountain speech, and the finger carefully followed the words. " 'I was decorated in 1917 by Clemenceau. It would be a betrayal of his memory and of the example of ardent patriotism he left us if I were to keep this decoration today.' " Cousin Perrin halted a moment, and looked gravely into Fenton's eyes. "You have read the terms of the decree of the thirteenth of September?" he said.

"Laval's order of mobilization," said Fenton. "That Frenchmen do forced labor for Germany."

"Yes," said Cousin Perrin, and his mouth was bitter. "This is the beginning. In the end, they will put them into German uniform," he said.

"No Frenchman will accept it!" said La Cousine, knitting savagely.

" 'It is impossible that liberty die in the country that gave it birth,' " said Cousin Perrin's strong, prophetic voice, and his finger followed Herriot's written words again. " 'It is impossible that liberty perish in the country from which it spread throughout the world.' In the great penitentiary which France has become," said Cousin Perrin, "these are the messages which we tap out on the walls of our cells to one another, and thus we know that other men are still alive."

He got to his feet now, and he looked from under the brim of his black hat at Fenton.

"Come with me. Have a look at the cheese room," he said.

He opened the door, and the jacket he had hung there swung out like a living thing, and the sleeve of it touched Fenton's arm and startled her as she followed him out of the kitchen and into the sun-dappled dark and cold. The windows were small as portholes in the stone of the walls, and she knew no eye could penetrate their dust, and yet as she looked at the glass of them, the singular uneasiness was there. *We're being asked to get out of Truex,* said de Vaudois' voice in a whisper in the room. *I have no intention of getting out—not until I've found out what it is they're trying to do.* There in the silence were the shelves as she had known them before, and the clean straw laid on them in readiness, but now shelf after shelf was empty, and the crocks for butter stood gaping on the floor.

"There is nothing," said Fenton, and there was sorrow in her voice as she thought of the richness of other years.

"No, nothing," said Cousin Perrin, but his dark eye gleamed on her face.

"If she has brought food to France, if she is serving too, then show her that we've not been idle," said La Cousine's voice. She stood tall and grim behind them in the doorway, and her hands were knitting still.

63

"Come, then," said Cousin Perrin again, and La Cousine stood aside to let them pass.

The cattle room opened from the kitchen as the cheese room and the bedroom did, and in winter the door stood open, so that the heat of the many cattle might serve to warm the house. There were stalls for thirty beasts in it, and as she walked the length of it with Cousin Perrin, Fenton saw that six of them were left. They stood stamping and lowing in their stalls, with their tails tied up for cleanliness to strings that hung from the beam above, and they turned their heads on their shoulders to watch the humans pass.

"It is nearly empty," Fenton said.

"Empty!" said Cousin Perrin, and he slapped a cow's lean haunches with the flat of his hand as he passed. "I have three more than I've the right to! I took them higher and kept them in the *sapins* when the commission came through."

He stopped at the last stall that stood bright with sun beneath the cobwebbed window, and the goat tethered to the wood of it waltzed to the end of her rope and turned to eye them there. Cousin Perrin stooped at once and slipped the rope from the little goat's neck and drove her out, free, into the passage.

"One goat! You had fifteen of them!" Fenton said.

"There are more," said Cousin Perrin. "I keep them higher."

Her eyes fled suddenly to the little window above their heads. It was filled with light, but for an instant it had seemed to her that a face was watching there. *I have no intention of getting out,* said de Vaudois' whisper across the sunlight and through the glass. *I have no intention of getting out until I've found out what they're trying to do.*

"Cousin Perrin, do not say these things aloud," she said, and she watched the window for the shadow of movement in it.

"I am afraid of no man," Cousin Perrin said.

He took the pitchfork from the corner of the stall now, and with the prongs of it he raked the straw and dung aside. When the flooring was free, and the boards lay bare before them, he set the pitchfork down. Then he stooped and raised one board from its place and laid it back along the stable wall.

"*Voilà*," he said, and he lifted and laid aside another. In a moment, the square opening lay completed at their feet. "They've passed this stall a dozen times, and the goat was always tied there, so they did not stop. They threw her a glance and went on," he said, and under his mustaches his lips seemed about to smile.

He went down first, and Fenton watched his hands gripping lower and lower on the ladder's rungs until she could no longer see them descending into the cavity of dark. And then, once he had reached the ground below, the unsteady flickering of a candle's light welled up the dark like water rising, and merged with the sunlight at the brink.

"Shall I come?" asked Fenton.

"Yes, come," said Cousin Perrin, and the sight of his face was lighted strong and clear below her, the lines deep in it, the eyes brilliant under the hat's brim, the pigment rich, like an oil portrait done by an old master hung suddenly there upon the dark. She went down the ladder to where he stood

65

on the hard-packed earth, and he lifted the candle a little in his hand. "*Voilà*," he said, and she looked in wonder at the shelves with the round little cakes of goat cheese stacked on them, and the milk standing in tall, cool crocks in the dampness, and the butter in the molds. "*Voilà*," said Cousin Perrin, "*voilà*," and his voice was unsteady as he said it, and Fenton looked quickly at him, and she saw there were tears upon his face. "Here it is," he said simply. "Here it is. All that we have to give, we give—but through what subterfuge, what trickery, what lies!" He raised the candle higher now, and the light of it sped farther into the dark, and revealed the shelves that lay beyond. "Eggs, butter, four kinds of cheese, goats' milk, cows' milk," he said softly, almost humbly to her. "There is wine, sugar, coffee, bread—everything that the country is going lean for want of."

"But how has it come here?" asked Fenton, scarcely aloud, and she looked at the stern, unbroken, tear-wet face in the candlelight, at the marvelously painted portrait of a grim-jawed, fearless man.

"The produce of the farm is ours," he said. "The fruit of the milk is ours. The other things are given to us."

"But why?" she whispered to him in wonder. "Why?"

"Because the mountain is hungry," said Cousin Perrin. "This is all we need to know."

"But this food? All this?" asked Fenton in stubborn bewilderment, and she made a gesture toward the shelves.

"It moves on to the frontier," said Cousin Perrin.

"But then it is contraband—contraband of war?" she said, not understanding yet.

66

"It is contraband," said Cousin Perrin, and there was something like exultation in his voice. "The glaciers are hungry. In a country of starving men, we are nourishing them at last."

"Do not speak so loudly of these things," said Fenton again. She lifted her head to the opening in the floor above them, and her hand fell on his arm. *If he was behind us in the square,* she thought, and for a moment she saw the scar as white as chalk across de Vaudois' face.

Cousin Perrin paused, listening with her, and then he shook his head.

"It is nothing," he said. "The cows stamping in their stalls." He looked at Fenton. "Besides there are ways—we are protected. It would not be wise to wander in the brush around the farm—"

In the kitchen, La Cousine was knitting still, and she looked up at Fenton in pride.

"You saw?" she asked.

"Yes," said Fenton. "I saw, but I do not know what it means."

"We do not need to know," said La Cousine. "It is like the knitting we have to do. There is merely the wool and the pattern to follow. Does the beast ask for reasons when the plowman gives him the way to go?" As she knitted, she made a gesture with her chin toward the package that lay on the table's boards. "There is the wool, and the words that go with it are: 'A mistake in the pattern is treason.'" Her voice was sharp with warning. "It would be as much treason," she said, "as if you spoke of what you have just seen below."

67

Fenton picked up the package of wool.

"Shall I bring the mittens here to you tomorrow, La Cousine?" she said.

"Give them to Jacqueminot," La Cousine said, knitting still. "He will be waiting for them tomorrow evening in the guides' café. You will put them into his hands yourself. You will not fail us."

"I will not fail you," said Fenton, and her voice was humble, and her eyes were fixed in promise on La Cousine's face.

It was on the way down the wagon trail that Fenton saw the little group of men coming up from below: five or six of them climbing up by the ice-edged stream, with packs on their backs and their ice axes thrust through the straps of them, and their ancient hats upon their heads. At the Calvary, where the trail forked, she stopped to watch them come. They must be setting off on a long excursion, she thought, for their packs were heavy—but this was not the season for long-distance going, nor was it the time to climb high in any season when the halo hung on Mont Blanc's brow. It was only as they took the last curve below her in the steep, rutted trail that she saw de Vaudois was among them. He was making use of his ice axe to aid him in the ascent, holding it like a city cane in the palm of one gloved hand. When he raised his head to glance before him, he saw her standing there ahead.

"Well, you see, I'm off!" he called up, speaking English to her, and the sound of it was carried down in the roar of the waterfall. She waited until they were nearly at the Calvary before she spoke.

68

"You haven't wasted any time," she said.

She saw he carried a lighter load than the others, and that there was a new little pheasant-feathered felt upon one side of his head. *The immaculate bourgeois still*, thought Fenton; *everything rigid and uneasy and new, and nothing casual, as a mountain man's things should be.*

"Just over twenty-four hours in the place, and I've already got it organized," he was saying. His breath came short, but his sharp, light eyes were filled with pleasure over whatever deal it was that he had just put through.

"Your weather's scarcely safe, is it?" she said when the party had stopped beside her. It was spoken to the guides, and spoken in French, and the oldest one, with the grizzled hair and the falcon-beaked nose, looked ahead at the sky.

"*B'en*, the stranger is in a hurry," he said, and it may have been irony that she heard in his voice. He shifted the rucksack on his back. "He hasn't long to stay," he said.

"It may hold twenty-four hours," said another of them, and Fenton saw the canvas sheet strapped to his pack. *To carry the mountain dead down in*, she thought, and the blood ran cold as glacier water in her heart.

"We'll go as far as we can," de Vaudois said, speaking a cheerful English still. In the unsparing light of day, she could see how deep was the white scar that slashed across his cheek and drew the corner of his mouth, as acid might have done. "I've got to get this business over with," he said. "The chap called Jacqueminot helped me out. He got back at noon, and in an hour he had a permit for me, signed by the *chef de brigade*, authorizing me to cross the glaciers, and supplies to

69

carry with me. So we're off," he said. "If bad weather catches us, we'll wait in a refuge until it clears——"

"I prefer to speak the language of the country," said Fenton. The guides, with the packs on their backs, and the ropes coiled at their waists, stood watching the two strangers with unflickering eyes. *They wait patient as mountains,* Fenton thought, *but their blood is impatient in them. Tourists are rare now, and it must be that he is paying them well to go.* "Did you go up with the search parties after the Swiss boy fell?" said Fenton to the old man with the falcon-face beneath the gray hat's brim.

"We were there. We were thirty-six hours looking for them," he said, using not night and day for time's dimensions, but the guides' scale of hours to describe it to her. "They broke the avalanche themselves, crossing at midday, when the snow was soft, and they went down with it."

De Vaudois glanced up now at the wooden cross that stood with its arms stretched open in anguish against the mountains and the sky.

"I've been hearing talk in the village of a miraculous Calvary," he said, speaking French, as if in amiable concession to Fenton now. "I'm interested in all these legends," he said, and his eyes were bright with satisfaction. *Because the thing I came here to accomplish is now on its way to accomplishment, I can touch on historical monuments, legends, superstitions,* said the look of complacency in his face. *You, my poor girl, are running futilely up and down the mountain after a man they tell you is dead, so I can afford to be generous with you. You prefer to speak French? Then French let it be. My mis-*

sion will be executed within the next few days, while to yours there is no issue. "Would this be your Miraculous Calvary?" he asked the waiting guides.

They looked at him, and they did not speak, and then the old guide shook his head.

"I've heard of no miracles," he said.

"Oh, come," said de Vaudois. "You hear the story in the village everywhere. They tell you there is a Calvary which men bring offerings to now." He looked from the guides to Fenton in amusement, then back to the guides again. "I've been told that *monsieur le curé* encourages the peasants to come even from the farthest villages in the plain below, walking all day to make pilgrimages to a Calvary that stands above Truex," he said. "Someone who swears he saw it with his own eyes tells me he has seen sugar carried up, and coffee, and loaves of bread, and even bottles of wine."

"Many stories are told to travelers," said Falcroz, the old guide. "Maybe you've heard the one of the white duck that you can see up there through the trees."

They turned their heads to where he pointed, and there in the rocky crags against the sky was the duck's shape drawn in snow in a gully between two horns of stone.

"What is the story of that?" said de Vaudois, and his eye went suddenly shrewd beneath his hat's crisp brim.

"If its head has melted by the end of May, then the summer will be long and hot," said Fenton to him. "And if its tail is still there by September, then winter will come early that year. Once," she said, looking at it, "the duck was gone by April. It had never been known to happen before."

71

"Yes," said another of the guides, and as he took the empty pipe from between his teeth, Fenton saw he was one of the two who had sat with Jacqueminot the night before in the guides' café. "You could see it melting from the village square, it went so fast."

"They say it was the tears of the guardian angels that washed it away," Falcroz said. "It is known that the guardian angels have second sight, and that was the spring the Boches invaded the country. The guardian angels saw them crossing the frontiers even before they came."

"*Quelle blague!*" said de Vaudois in ridicule.

"Yes, like the story of the food brought to the Calvary," said Falcroz, looking toward the heights.

The food, thought Fenton, and she saw the shelves and the crocks and the molds beneath the stable flooring.

"Oh, come," said de Vaudois, insisting on it. "I've heard that men will carry half a loaf of bread thirty kilometers to lay it down on the Calvary steps. They've told me that peasants save coffee grain by grain until they've collected enough to bring it——"

"*B'en*, if that's the truth, let's lie in wait for them and take it from them!" Falcroz said, and the other guides laughed aloud.

"The story goes that men and women, and children even," de Vaudois went on, "will kneel down and make a feint of praying while they lay their offerings here." He gestured toward the Cross. "And by morning there'll be nothing left——"

"*B'en*," said the old guide, "would it be that the guardian angels are feeling the restrictions too, and that human beings are pinching and saving for them?"

But de Vaudois had had enough of it now, and of the sound of them laughing aloud, and he looked ahead impatiently.

"We'll be getting on our way," he said shortly to them.

"*Bonne montée,*" said Fenton.

"*Bonne descente,*" said the guides, and she started down the slope of the wagon trail while the others took the right-hand fork above the waterfall, and crossed through the shallows there, and began the climb toward snow.

The weather held that night, and the next day there was little color left in the sky, and the air was warm, and Fenton went out onto the bedroom balcony and sat knitting in the sun. The mountains were clear as glass above, with the snow turned bluish on them, and edged—as they are before the weather's break—with a strong, bright thread of indigo. Below in the hotel garden, the telescope was tipped on its tripod between the trees, its funnel pointing upward, and the garden chairs were stacked for winter still against the garage wall. Fenton kept the pattern of the mitten on her knee before her, and now she looked up from it to the sound of footsteps crossing the gravel below.

"I was going to see if I could catch sight of the Swiss and his party through the glass," said Madame Perrin. Over the balcony's rail, Fenton could see her in the purple sweater with the skirt drawn tight across the hips—the hair in curlpapers still, the heels of her cheap, strapped slippers high.

"They probably are on the glacier now," said Fenton, and

73

she knitted the black and the white, and the white and the black, in the mitten's pattern.

Madame Perrin lifted one short arm in the purple sleeve, and with her soiled, plump hand she touched the ends of her hair.

"I've been trying to get to the coiffeur for a week," she said. "I always think hotel guests like coming to a place where the lady keeps herself looking nice. Monsieur de Vaudois was saying yesterday that it's always a brunette you read about in history, never a blonde." Madame Perrin's shoulders were heavy and stooped, and an inch of white hair lay at her temples and her brow, but when she talked of the Swiss there was something girl-like in her face. "His business takes him around," she said. "I don't know if he's mentioned it to you—it's jewelry, watches." She stood looking up at Fenton on the balcony in the sun. "He was kind enough to say that he'd like to send me a souvenir back from Geneva," she said. "I don't know if it would be a wristwatch, or a bracelet, or a brooch, or what." And *What does he want of her*, thought Fenton, *that he sits in the café and talks of sending her presents, and of the beauty of her hair?* "I should think I could accept it from him, married or not," said Madame Perrin, and she looked up, smiling like a girl. "I've told Gustav that if we make things nice for him, he'll come back and bring compatriots with him for the skiing season. I should think I could accept a little something without it causing too much talk——"

"You'll be making Gustav jealous," said Fenton, knitting.

74

"Ah, Gustav!" Madame Perrin cried out in irritation. "He went and had himself made a prisoner for a year, and now he's stuck in the post office all day! I haven't as much as a cat to talk to out of season——"

"That's because they've all been eaten," Fenton said.

"Monsieur de Vaudois is someone to sit in the café with and talk to for an hour," said Madame Perrin. She turned to the telescope now, and she swung its eye upward to focus on the high, cold slopes of snow. "He likes to hear about this and that, about all the stories that are going around," she said, and Fenton's needles halted a moment. *The Miracle of the Calvary,* said the silence. "We were talking about *monsieur le curé,*" said Madame Perrin, "and I said I thought the Church, at least, should keep out of politics."

"The curé?" said Fenton in a quiet voice, and she waited.

"It's no secret that the village doesn't go to Mass to save its soul any more, but to get the news since the law about the foreign broadcasts," said Madame Perrin. Her back was turned to the balcony as she spoke, her eye fixed to the telescope's glass. "The curé gets the English broadcasts during the week, and delivers them on Sunday from the pulpit. Gustav goes to Mass now instead of to the *bistro.* He understands the code terms, or whatever it is. I went once and couldn't make head or tail of it." Madame Perrin turned the long, delicate barrel of sight across the heights of snow. "There's a wind up there," she said. "The peaks are smoking."

"The peasants say the weather will break," said Fenton, and she knitted fast.

75

By evening the pair of mittens was done, and now the rain had begun to fall. Fenton put on her climbing boots, and buttoned her blue-gray coat across, and knotted a handkerchief over her hair, and she walked quickly down the cobbled streets to the dark heart of the town. The street lamps were not lit yet, and the clock in the steeple marked half-past five. The torrent of water sped full and loud beneath the bridge, and she crossed it, running. The wind was blowing hard, and the rain slapped like a wet cloth on her face as she opened the door of the guides' café. After the cold of the night, the air inside was warm, and the lamp burned under the center beam, but the tables stood empty. She closed the door behind her, and she crossed the flagstones quickly to the kitchen's light. The old man, the blue, carpenter's apron knotted at his waist, was standing by the stove.

"I have to see Jacqueminot," she said, and her breath came fast. The old man turned and looked at her with gentle, red-rimmed eyes.

"Come to the fire," he said. "Your face is wet."

"It's from the rain," she said.

"Tomorrow it will be snow," he said, and he passed his veined, unsteady hand across his eyes.

"Has Jacqueminot come in yet?" Fenton said, and she took off her gloves and spread her hands before the heat. She waited another moment, her hands open, before she said: "Père Chatelard, I must see Jacqueminot."

"Because of the weather, he set off early tonight," the old man said. "He left a quarter of an hour before you came."

76

"He's gone!" said Fenton. "Then I'll have to catch him up. I'll have to do it."

"His pack was heavy," old Chatelard said. "He'll climb slowly because he has far to go."

"Does he go by the Calvary?" asked Fenton, and she pulled her gloves quickly on again. The old man bent to put more wood into the stove's mouth, and then he lifted the saucepan's lid with the wooden spoon, and his seemingly blinded eyes peered under at what was cooking on the flame.

"He goes by the other way. He goes by Les Mouilles," he said, and *Les Mouilles*, she thought, *Les Mouilles*, and she saw Cousin Perrin in the farmhouse again, stooping above the ash. *Les Mouilles*, said the echo of Cousin Perrin's voice, loud, prophetic, clear. *Ravanel set up the mountain toward Les Mouilles one day at dawn with a pack on his back, and we never heard of him again. One by one, they have gone from us*, echoed Cousin Perrin's voice; *one by one, one by one, they go.* "The path he takes runs through Les Mouilles and passes the refuge at the corniche," old Chatelard said, and Fenton, running now, took the sound of it with her out the café door.

The rain and wind were savage in the street, and she walked with her head down, and the wet streamed down her face like tears. *He can't have got far on a night like this,* she said to the dark. *He'll be going slowly. Once out of the town when I start climbing, I'll hear his steps on the rocks ahead. I'll catch him up by the old ski jump, or lower even. Oh, damn the wind. La Cousine, I won't fail you,* she said. But

77

once she had left the town and started the slope through the pine trees in the dark, the echo of Cousin Perrin's voice was heard again. *One by one, they have gone from us,* it said through the wildness of the night. *They go with packs on their backs, in darkness. One by one, they go.*

Fenton passed the ski jump, knowing it merely by the feel of the land. *A little higher now, to the right,* she thought, *the abandoned farm will lie.* The stones slipped sideways under her feet, and the wind drove down through the trees, and their branches moved in tumult. She felt the wet on her head and shoulders, soaking cold through the scarf's stuff and the blue coat's wool. *In ten minutes, I'll pass by the houses of Les Mouilles,* she thought, and her head was lowered against the cold, dark, slapping fury of the storm. *On the left there will be the chapel, and the stations of the cross, and the dogs will come out of the houses and bark at me as I pass. And it may be there that I'll hear Jacqueminot's steps on the road ahead.* But the houses of Les Mouilles were shuttered against the night, and the dogs stayed in by the fires and did not stir, and there was no sound of any man making his way up the path in the dark. *In a minute I'll pass the ruins of the tavern,* she thought, but her legs ached now from the rapid going, and the skirts of her coat clung heavy with wet to her knees. *I'll not fail you, La Cousine,* she said; *I'll catch him up—only it may not have been this way that he came, it may not have been this path at all.*

The ruins of the tavern were there; the summer it had burned all night they had seen it from below. That had been the Fourteenth of July, and everyone in the village was dancing under the lanterns on the square, and the conflagration of the tavern was suddenly there on the heights above, like a caldron of red-hot metal laid open to the sky. Because of the wine they'd drunk or the day it was, no one believed in the sight of disaster for a little while; and they had drunk more wine and danced the harder until the bells in the chapel of Les Mouilles cried down the mountain in despair, and the Truex church bells answered. And in spite of the state they were in, the men had had to run for their firemen's hats and their lengths of hose and stagger up the mountain.

But whatever had happened that night had been part of the celebration, thought Fenton as she climbed. The hose had twisted around the pine trees when they carried it up, and nothing could free it, for one man would reel up the slope and another down it, taking the opposite ends of it with him. Everything had been something to laugh yourself sick about in other years: the pails that Virgil, the humpback, carried had crashed with him into the ravine; and Dizot, the fire chief, found out when he was halfway up that he'd lost his gold-buckled belt on the way, and he wouldn't go up to the fire without it. They'd left him on his hands and knees, feeling the ground in the dark for it under the needle trees.

And what had they found when they got to the burning tavern that night? *When we walked in,* was how Bastineau told it, and they laughed for a week, *the peasants playing belote were sitting at the tables still and even if the roof was gone and the attic burning, nothing would make them stir. The tavernkeeper and his wife were carrying the chairs and tables out of the café, but the men wouldn't put their cards*

79

down! It was a national holiday to them, and on national holidays you played belote and drank red wine and lost all the money you had, and a fire was absolutely nothing. *It was merely another part of the celebration,* Fenton thought, *just as everything was part of some kind of celebration before war came.* The fire was nothing at all until the beams in the tavern room began smoldering above their heads, and the water from the buckets of the fire brigade spilled on the brims of their hats as they played.

And where are the firemen of Les Mouilles? Bastineau had shouted as he carried a spinning wheel and a cradle out. *They're in there playing belote!* said the tavernkeeper, and only when the back of the house was gone did they take up their bottles and glasses and the hands that had just been dealt them and stagger out. And there they sat down in the summer night at the tables that had been salvaged, and they went on playing in the fire's glow.

Fenton splashed through running water in the dark now as the stream cut suddenly swift across the path. She was out of Les Mouilles, and climbing again through forest, and here the mountain's shoulder broke the fury of the wind, and her breath was short in her mouth from going fast. But *I'll not give it up,* she said in silence; *I've got this far and in a minute I'll hear the twigs breaking or the stones sliding down under Jacqueminot's feet.* There was another half-hour of it, and now the sound of the falling rain had altered, and she knew that it had turned to snow. *And why are you hurrying after him like this,* spoke the cold in her veins; *to give him a pair of mittens that he perhaps doesn't know is missing? And of what importance are these mittens? Will the end of the world come if the sixth pair isn't in his hands?* And then she remembered the refuge. It must be close now, to the right of the path—the log hut where the sleds to bring down the injured were kept and where the three-leggèd stove stood in the center of the room. There might be dry wood stacked up behind the stove, and matches to light it. And suddenly—as if someone had silently opened a door wide in the dark—she knew that the clearing before the hut stood open in the trees.

The wind swept bitterly down the mountain here and struck hard at her face, and she lowered her head against the driving snow. *I will stay just a little while,* she thought, and her heavy boot struck the timber step, and her numb hand fumbled for the latch. Even as she pushed the door in, the dream of warmth and sleep possessed her. It entered her veins; it spread like a deep-colored wine in her icy blood; it softened her eyes with promise, so that once she stood inside the room she accepted without question what was there. She stood without wonder in its light, felt its warmth on her flesh, knew—as if having dreamed it once—that Jacqueminot, with his pack laid aside, would stand up from the bench by the stove and face her in surprise.

Three

"Is THIS coincidence?" Jacqueminot asked quietly.

He wore the lumberjack shirt, and the silver-studded belt was buckled at his narrow waist, and the dark climbing trousers were fastened just below the knee. There was no snow on his boots, merely the dark ring of wet staining the timber where he stood. *So he must have been here some time*, she thought; it had been long enough for the air in the room to heat, and for the snow to have melted from his shoe leather and from the folds of his wind jacket that lay across the chair.

82

"No," said Fenton, and she pushed the door closed against the wind. "I followed you up here."

She heard her own words spoken across the room of the mountain hut, heard them in separate and remote articulation, as if another person had said them aloud. Jacqueminot stood by the hot little iron stove, and his eyes in his pointed, faunlike face were quick and dark and troubled.

"There's no reason good enough to bring you out on a night like this," he said.

The snow was dripping now from the handkerchief tied across her hair, and the wet ran down her brow and cheeks, and she lifted one hand and wiped the drops away.

"I thought it was," she said, and for an instant the room swung slowly in the heat. "I thought I would catch you lower down." She tried to take her gloves off, but her fingers were still numb. "I didn't mean to come this far," she said.

It might have been then that he saw for the first time the look of weariness in her eyes, or heard the unsteadiness in her voice, for he made a motion toward the bench.

"Come and sit down," he said, but his voice was hard and he did not move from where he stood. "It's your good luck that the shoulder strap of my rucksack broke. I stopped in here to patch it up."

She crossed the room and sat down on the bench, and leaned toward the heat of the stove for a moment. Then she took off her gloves and spread them, wet, on the bench beside her, and she unknotted the handkerchief that covered her head. When she shook her hair back, the drops from it hissed as they struck the stove.

"I had to bring you the pair of mittens. I had to do that," she said. She took them from her pocket and laid them on the wood of the bench. "La Cousine said there had to be six. I knew it mattered for what you have to do."

"La Cousine said you would bring them to the guides' café," Jacqueminot said, and he did not move. "When you didn't come, I picked up a sixth pair from one of the peasant women on the way." He thrust his hands down into his trousers' pockets now, and he paced back and forth a moment between the table and the stove. Then he stopped short and faced her. "Have you any idea what you're getting into?" he said.

"I've been trying to put things together," said Fenton. She did not look up when she spoke, but sat with her hands spread toward the stove. "I haven't got very far."

"You've got this far," said Jacqueminot, and he gave a short, quick laugh. He sat down on the table's edge, his hands in his trousers' pockets, his eyes on her as she leaned toward the stove. "The thing I mistrust about it is," he said, "how far you intend to go."

The loose, light hair fell across the side of her face, and she looked musingly at her ringless fingers spread before her toward the heat.

"If I told you I was lost, it might sound a bit absurd," she said. And then she straightened up, and lifted her head to look at him, and the hair fell back upon her shoulders. "Oh, I don't mean lost in the mountains—not in that sense," she said to the dark, quick, faunlike face across the room, and to the tense look in his eyes. "There is an expression for it—*perdre le nord*. That's what's happened to me for the moment. I think I lost it when you said to me what you did in the train—and I'm still trying to find it."

"You might make it clearer," said Jacqueminot, and he took his pipe from his pocket and set it between his teeth.

"Well, suppose," said Fenton quietly, and she looked at her open hands again, "suppose you knew exactly where the North Star was, and had always known it. Ever since you were a child, suppose you knew what part of the sky to look for it in, and it was always there. And then suddenly when you turned to the same place to find it, it wasn't there any longer. It simply wasn't there where it had always been, and you swung around to the east and the west and every which way, looking for it." She put her hair, long and light and wet still from the rain, back behind her ears. "That's the way I feel about Bastineau being gone," she said.

Jacqueminot lit the sulphur match with the nail of his thumb, and waited, before setting the flame to his pipe, for the odor to perish from the air.

"This kind of thing will get you into trouble—serious trouble—danger," he said.

Fenton sat silent a moment, looking down at the side of her mountain boot, and then—as if in willful retraction of all she had said in emotion to him—she said abruptly:

"The sole of it's going."

Jacqueminot sat with his leg swinging from the table's edge.

"You won't be able to buy others," he said.

"When I get to our chalet, I'll find a pair or two there," Fenton said, and she ran her finger under the broken sole. "I started two days ago, but I didn't make it. I saw La Cousine and knitted the mittens instead."

Jacqueminot crossed the room and picked up the pair of mittens from the bench then. He stood with his pipe in his teeth a moment, studying the pattern in the wool.

"You're not afraid of mountains, and you're not afraid of men," he said, as if it was this they had been speaking of. "Whether it's because you know them well or not well enough, I haven't yet made out. But this year they've changed—both men and mountains. They've changed. They're fiercer, more relentless," he said, and the sound of threat was there.

"I've known these mountains and the men who climb them a long time," said Fenton.

"Not all of us," said Jacqueminot. He walked back to the table, and he unbuckled a side pocket of his rucksack that stood, packed full, upon the table. "I, for one, am a stranger to you. And there is de Vaudois," he said, and he put the mittens in.

"You don't trust the man," she said, musing on it. "And yet you got him the guides and the permit to go up to the avalanche."

"The quicker he does what he came here to do, the quicker he'll go," said Jacqueminot.

"And you send him up with the weather changing," she said, as if in reflection to the stove.

86

"The guides know their business," said Jacqueminot. "He was in a hurry. They'll turn back now that the weather's changed."

And then, as if she could stand no more of subterfuge, Fenton said abruptly:

"What are you trying to keep from us—from de Vaudois and from me?"

Jacqueminot stooped and picked up a short, square-cut log from behind the stove, and he raised the iron ring with the poker's beak, and dropped it in on the flame.

"You and de Vaudois," he said, and he did not look at her. "You came here together. It is possible, even, that you were not strangers on the train." He thrust the log into place with the poker, and stooped for another. "We have too much to lose," he began, and Fenton cried out:

"I never saw him before that night! You know it!"

"Isn't it plain enough what we're doing?" he asked, and he stood there looking down at her. "Isn't it clear that there aren't many ways left for a Frenchman to pick up his living in times like these? We do it however we can—a skein of wool here, a pound of butter there, a pair of mittens somewhere else. My pack here is filled with contraband," he said, and he motioned toward the table with the pipe held in his hand. "You're French, partly French," he said, and his eyes were asking the promise of her. "You've lived here—you're one of us. I'm hoping to God the same means won't be needed to stop you as we've used to stop the others. I'm taking your word of honor for granted," he said.

"My word of honor!" said Fenton, and she looked in amusement at him. "But half the village is in on it, whatever it is!"

"De Vaudois isn't," said Jacqueminot, and his eyes were grave.

"He told me of the Miracle of the Calvary. He knows that much," said Fenton, and as she lifted her head the light hair fell across her cheek again.

"People talk," said Jacqueminot in impatience. He knocked the ashes from his pipe against the side of the stove. "As for the Calvary, we've nothing to lose," he said, "if what de Vaudois knows ends there."

"So it's black market, purely and simply," said Fenton, after a moment, her voice musing, quiet, her hands hanging warm and lax now between her knees. *And what has this to do with remaining a Frenchman,* she thought, *and with all the other fine things that Jacqueminot said about his country's soil? What has this to do with the vision in La Cousine's eyes, or with Cousin Perrin repeating in the prophet's voice: "We've lost Socquet, Ravanel, Couttet; we've lost Durand, Sabrone, and Bastineau."* "You know, I had illusions about you at first," she said slowly after a moment. "But now I wonder why you're contemptuous of de Vaudois, after all. He has his business in Switzerland—you have yours on the frontier. He's bourgeois, mercenary, neutral. What are you?"

"Not neutral!" said Jacqueminot in a fierce, low voice. "There isn't a neutral left in France!"

"But smuggling!" said Fenton, and she put her hair back on her shoulders again, and she laughed a little. Then she looked at the rucksack on the table. "Rather me than the Italians on the other side. If you've got food in there, rather me than the Fascisti. I'm hungry," she said.

Jacqueminot opened the tightly laced mouth of the rucksack now, and for the first time he smiled.

"I'll charge it up to bribery," he said as he laid the food out on the table's boards.

He cut the bread, holding the great half loaf of it against his heart, cutting it thickly and generously toward him, the crust of it breaking crisply, and Fenton went quickly to the table and scooped into her hand the crumbs that fell.

"Butter!" she said, with the crumbs in her mouth. She stood looking in wonder at it. "Real butter!" And: "Ham!" she said in another moment: "Ham!" as he laid it on the slice of bread.

"There's cheese to follow," he said, and he handed the bread to her. She waited a moment, marveling at the delicate slice that lay fresh and rosy on it.

"Cheese!" she said, as he took the paper from it. Her cheek was swollen as she chewed. "You mean—just to look at? Certainly you're not going to cut it! I don't believe it!" she said.

"There's one thing I'd give a year of my life for," said Jacqueminot. He cut the cheese paper-thin and laid the sliver on the second piece of bread. "A *fondu*," he said. "I can see the steaming casserole of it set down before us here—right here," he said, and he hastened to clear the space for it on the table. Then he put his head back and closed his eyes as if to breathe the incredible pungence of it in. "Half a bottle of kirsch, a glass of cognac, a dash of Cointreau———"

"You'd better stir it!" said Fenton, playing the game with him now. "Don't let it stick and burn——"

"Burn?" Jacqueminot cried out, and he picked up the imaginary spoon and leaned above the table. "It's thickening," he said. "Pass the croutons and let's begin."

"It smells of heaven," Fenton said.

"Put a crouton on your fork and dip it in," said Jacqueminot, and he moved around the table. "I'll get the salad and uncork the wine."

"Get your fork and dip in too," said Fenton, and he stood there looking at the side of her face as she leaned above the dish that wasn't there.

"I've started to make the dressing," he said, but he did not move. "Oh, olive oil and sliced tomatoes! It's been three years," he said.

"Look," said Fenton suddenly. She turned to look at him, the good fresh bread and the cheese gone tasteless in her mouth now. "There's something wrong with the game we're playing. I mean, I'm eating a sandwich I can touch and bite," she said, and she held out what remained of it. "You're eating *fondu* and salad, and there doesn't happen to be any. That isn't the way the game's meant to be played."

"I ate before starting up," said Jacqueminot, and she looked at the narrow, pointed face from which the humor and youth had been abruptly wiped away. "I'm not hungry. I've got my rucksack full there if I wanted to eat," he said.

"Except you won't take it for yourself," she said, and she held the sandwich from her now, as if it were a guilty and offensive thing.

"I'm having *fondu* and sliced tomatoes," said Jacqueminot, and he smiled at her. "Watch your hair!" he cried out quickly then, and she started back. "It's too beautiful to burn," he said.

He sat down on the table's edge, his arms folded, looking soberly at her.

"I believed you for a second," she said, and she put her hair back on her shoulders, and she did not laugh. "I believed there was a spirit lamp lighted there on the table, and a saucepan of *fondu* steaming on it, and that my hair might catch fire if I leaned too near——"

And I believed the other thing, too, she said in silence. *I may have been crazy, but for a split second I believed that too. I believed it was possible that you carried food up to the frontier merely to sell it to whoever would pay the best price for it. But it isn't for money that you'd sit hungry here while you dream the credible dreams of food set on the table before you. It isn't from avarice that you'd spare me so little to eat with a rucksack full of it standing there. I've seen you offer your last cigarettes to strangers in a train, and I've heard you say: "In times like these, men do not exchange their native soil for another unless they are driven to it." It's not for money that your eyes are hollow, and that your skin is drawn fleshless across your bones.*

In a moment, he glanced at the watch on his wrist, and then he stood up, and shook out his legs, and he jerked his belt a hole tighter.

"It's after ten. I'll be getting on," he said.

"It's a bad night to go high," said Fenton, and she watched

91

him take the waterproof jacket from the chair and slip his head and shoulders through.

"I'll break the climb farther on," he said. His arms struggled through the wind jacket's sleeves, and he laced it fast at the hips and neck. "I've got the shelter of the woods for another half-hour," he said, and then he stopped. "What about you?" he said. "Can you make it down?"

"I could do it with my eyes closed in any weather," she said, but Jacqueminot shook his head.

He was hooded like a deep-sea diver, accoutered and helmeted for his element, and he moved in masked and heavy-booted courage now as if to the water's edge. When he opened the door, the light from the refuge cut bright as a knife across the falling snow without, and the wind drove with a little cry into the refuge room.

"It's drifting deep," he said. It took both hands to close the door again against the wind. "You'd do better to stay here until morning," he said. "There's wood to keep you warm."

"I'll stay," she said quietly. "There's only this," she said, and her voice stopped for a moment. "It's Bastineau," she said. "I mean—if there's any hope, if there's any chance——"
Jacqueminot stood pulling the sealskin mittens on, and then he backed to the table's edge, and he flexed his knees to hook his arms through the rucksack's straps, and he jerked the weight of it to his back. Then he straightened up, unbalanced a little by the load. "I mean, maybe you could start believing that I'm with you by this time," Fenton said.

Now that he was ready to go, he turned near the door and spoke to her again.

"I don't know if you remember the first words you ever said to me," he said, and he stood there, half crippled by the rucksack's weight. "You were sitting opposite me in the dark, and I hadn't seen your face yet. I didn't know what you looked like then, but you said: 'I was brought up in these mountains,' and because of your way of saying it, I wanted at once then to believe in you. I want to believe in you now," he said, and his eyes were uneasy. "But this is a desperate thing we're doing. If people interfere, there's only one way to deal with them. We can't take any chances. That's why I ask this of you: for Bastineau's sake, keep out of the mountains. For the love of every mountain man, alive or dead, keep silent about us and go away."

He went to the door, the deep-sea diver moving toward his element again, and he opened it and walked out into the crying wind and the dark. And for a little while after the door had closed behind him, a handful of spray lay drying on the floor.

By morning the wind had fallen, but the sky was as heavy as iron, and little particles of snow hung, as if caught frozen, on the air. Before the door of the refuge, there was no blemish on the white—no footstep, twig, not even a fallen pine cone marred it. Fenton stepped out into its pure, still depths and it broke, foamlike, above her knees. There was no sign or sound of life in the stillness, and her steps were muffled as she moved

93

off from the refuge and down through the perfect silence of the weighted trees. It was early in the day, and she would go to the chalet, she thought, and let the light and air in, and find a pair of boots to wear. She put her hand in the pocket of her coat, and the chalet key was there, and—like the sole survivor of the violence of the night—she broke the snow in deep, soft footfalls, descending the path that nothing delineated except the strip of open sky that followed overhead.

She went fast, sliding down through the trees, leaving the forest behind her, and then the houses of Les Mouilles behind her, with the sound of the dogs that had come out to bark at her dying far now over the fields of snow. She came to the swinging, log bridge above the icebound ravine, and her foot in the shoe with the broken sole was cold and wet as she walked across it. At the next turn, she would see the chalet that was home—the sloping eaves of it, and the balconies running the house's length, and the oil-stained railings carved in the shape of lifted stag heads with the antlers edged with snow. *It will be cold as the tomb inside, after three years of no fires lit*, she thought, *but it will be home still, with the books on the shelves, and the old coats in the closets, and the flower prints from the Paris quays still hanging on the walls.*

And suddenly the needle trees stood apart before it, and the valley spread open below, as if in homage, with range after cold, blue range of mountains dropping icily away. Here was the shape of home—the carved shutters bolted against the weather and intruders, here the granite step of the house, and here the iron knocker, and Fenton's heart beat quickly in her blood as she took the key from her pocket and set it in the

94

lock. *There used to be words that I said aloud, like a charm, before I went in or out. If I said them before I went in, it meant there'd be chocolate soufflé for supper that night, and once it made fresh pineapples come from Paris when we didn't expect them at all. And if I said the words going out, it meant the skiing would be good, or that the ferrets would turn white early. Or it meant that I'd be lucky enough to see Bastineau coming up or down the road.*

"*J'ai fait trois fois le tour du monde,*" she said aloud now for luck, and she turned the key in the lock, and pushed open the nail-studded door.

The hall was paved with stone, and the rack for the skis stood to the left. The snow-white light of day came in for a moment through the door, and when Fenton closed it behind her, the half-dark dropped like a curtain across the length of the hall and the curve of the stairs she knew. She touched the electric button by the great carved chest, but no light sprang into the bulb in the rustic lantern overhead. The switch was in there where the coats used to hang for any kind of weather, she knew, and she opened the door of what they had called the waxing room, where the skins had hung and the ski waxes stood on the shelves—this one for spring snow, and this for powder snow, and this varnish or the other for the heaviest snow that fell. But as she groped in the clothes closet for the switch's handle, she wondered a moment, for she felt no coats against her hand. Her fingers found and lifted the switch, and the lights went on in the waxing room and the hallway. As she turned, she heard the knocking of what might have been a shutter blown loose at the back of

95

the chalet, above the ravine, and she saw the person turning toward her from the other wall.

"You frightened me," she said aloud to the bareheaded girl in the blue-gray coat who faced her from the full-length glass.

The shelf where the ski waxes had stood was empty, and there were no ski boots or climbing boots or crampons standing, as they had always stood, upon the shelves below. The skins were gone from the pegs on the walls, and the closets were empty. The place was as stripped as if nothing had ever waited there to be laced or strapped or buckled on for action.

"The coats are gone, and the boots are gone," she said, and the girl in the mirror shook back her hair. "Perhaps we packed them away upstairs, and I've forgotten," she said aloud, and then she saw the paper that lay folded just inside the cupboard door.

There was nothing in any way singular about the paper, and for the first moment that she opened it, she stood looking without recognition at the writing it bore. She had read it through twice, shaping the words with her lips as if to give them substance, before she began to think: *This is his writing. That is his initial at the bottom of the page.* There were the strong, bold characters of his hand—the salutation, the words of the message, the single letter standing at the close.

MONSIEUR RAVEL:
   We have broken into your house. Here is the memorandum of what we have taken away.
      4 pairs of ski boots
      3   "   of climbing boots

96

3   "   of crampons
4   "   of seal skins
3   "   of skis
2   "   of metal sticks, various waxes and varnishes,
          now unobtainable, and indispensable to our needs
3 ski jackets
2 loden capes, with hoods
3 wind jackets

You will understand why we have done this, and not condemn us. Frenchmen are in need of these things. Frenchmen will make use of them, to the end that every Frenchman may be liberated to live, to think, to work, to act in dignity and in security.

Respectfully,
B.

He has been here. He is alive then, she said in silence, and she stood quiet a moment, simply holding the piece of paper in her hand. And then she was suddenly out in the snow again, and the door was locked behind her, and she was running fast down the road, with the key of the chalet in her coat pocket, and the paper folded tight and small in her ungloved fingers, as warm to her flesh as if it were alive. The roofs of the village houses were just below now, with the snow deep on them, and the church steeple stood tall and delicate and high in the morning light. She went quickly through the streets, past the shopwindows, across the bridge with the torrent beneath it, past the pump at the corner with the curly beard of ice frozen beneath its mouth. When she came to the mayor's house, she ran up the stone steps of it, and she pulled the bell, and she heard it ring aloud within. It was Jeanne-Marie who opened the door and who stood, with a little shawl over her shoulders, facing her with dark, relentless eyes.

"Ah, Fenton," she said, but there was no greeting in it. She held the little shawl around her with one hand. "What is it?" she said, but she might have been saying: *So you are not gone yet! I said it plainly enough the first night to you! Do you still refuse to understand?*

"I have to talk to you," said Fenton quickly, and the girl standing in the doorway seemed to close her lips on what she had been about to say, and instead she shook her head. "But you can't have changed so completely to me!" cried Fenton in a quick, low voice. "We were friends, Jeanne-Marie! You can't refuse five minutes' talk with me!"

"There is scarcely the time for social calls this year," said Jeanne-Marie. In her eyes there was no sign of mitigation, and her mouth was narrow and hard with pain.

"But there's time for the truth!" said Fenton quickly.

"Ah, the truth!" repeated Jeanne-Marie, and the mockery in her voice was clear. "The Americans have several versions of it as far as we French are concerned," she said. "It is perhaps with Vichy that you want to speak. We are outlaws. We have no standing."

Fenton took her hand from her coat pocket then, and the paper was in it. She opened it hastily, furtively out, and Jeanne-Marie saw the writing across it, and the single letter standing at the close.

"Come in," she said then, under her breath. She said it quietly and steadily, but her eyes had filled with trepidation. "In the name of God," she repeated, "come in."

98

She had opened the door wider, and Fenton followed her down the unheated passageway into the kitchen's warmth, where the only fire in the house was lit, and Jeanne-Marie pulled a chair forward to the stove.

"Sit down. Tell me where you got the note," she said, speaking quickly.

"I went to the chalet for the first time since I returned," Fenton began. She sat down and pulled her coat open. "I needed a change of shoes," she said, her voice a little breathless, and she looked down at the side of her broken shoe.

"And the note?" said Jeanne-Marie. She spoke in a low, tense voice, and her face and her throat were as smooth as wax as she stood with her arms folded, watching Fenton. She was dressed in black, with the black shawl over her shoulders, and a silver brooch held the white collar at her neck—a brooch on which was curved the hunting horn of the Alpine Infantry. "Where did you find the note?" she said. The dark braids shaped a crown high on her head, and her brow was scarred with her concern.

"It was there," said Fenton. "At the chalet. In the down-stairs cupboard."

"Written to you?" said Jeanne-Marie.

"To my father," Fenton said.

"What does it say? I saw only the writing," said Jeanne-Marie, and now she brought a chair close to Fenton's, and she sat down. "We must talk quietly. One is never safe. We might be overheard," she said.

"It is not what he says," said Fenton, and she opened it out

99

in her fingers again. "It is simply that he wrote it, and if he wrote it, then he isn't——"

"Hush," said Jeanne-Marie. "Let me see it," she said, and she took it from Fenton's hand and spread it carefully on her knee. Fenton leaned toward her now, and the two women read it in silence together.

"There it is," said Fenton when she was done. "Men lost in the schrund don't need these things," she said in a low voice, and the blood ran cold with wonder in her. "It's only living men who need boots and skis and crampons to take them where they want to go."

"Yes," said Jeanne-Marie after a moment, and her eyes were calm, and nothing had altered in her face. "He needed them when he wrote that—that is certain. But there's no date to it," she said. "It might have been written any year—the winter of 1939, for instance, before the armistice." She turned the paper over as if seeking some indication on it. "He wrote that, Fenton, when he was still with the Alpine Infantry on the frontier."

"No," said Fenton quickly, "he wrote it when he had no uniform to wear any longer. He wrote it when he, and the others like him, were taking what rags and scraps they could to cover them to fight for France!"

Jeanne-Marie looked at her quietly a moment, and then she shook her head.

"But you know the story," she said wearily. "We all know it. I'll tell it to you again if you wish to hear. Bastineau and two others——"

"Only it isn't true!" Fenton cried out. "He was never

100

killed on the glacier! I have the proof of it now in his own writing in my hand!"

Jeanne-Marie made a gesture for silence.

"But you do not know when that was written."

"Yes! It is dated!" Fenton cried softly out. "Oh, not with numerals, Jeanne-Marie, but by the words he has written! He was alive and confiscating things Frenchmen needed in a year when Frenchmen had nothing! I have been away a long time, but I have listened to every word that was uttered! Don't you think I know those words as well as I know the syllables of my name? 'So that every Frenchman may be liberated to live, to think, to work, to act in dignity and in security.' " Jeanne-Marie looked quickly about them. "They are de Gaulle's words! They were spoken in 1941!" said Fenton. "Don't you think I know how they have been carried like a promise in Frenchmen's hearts?"

"Hush!" whispered Jeanne-Marie. "If you know these things, be still then!"

But now Fenton's cheeks were hot, and she spoke with passion.

"The peasants have taken me back, Jeanne-Marie, as the mountains take one back, without question or suspicion! Virgil and Dizot, and Père Chatelard, they have given me their hands as friends, and only you are on your guard! Cousin Perrin and La Cousine can sit at table with me and speak of the ways that men can serve——"

"Wait!" said Jeanne-Marie quietly. "You did not return simply among us, Fenton. We who bear the burden of it all must suspect if the others are too simple to. You did not come

101

back alone," she said, the words spoken clearly and exactly, but scarcely above a whisper, "and you came back with a purpose. You came back with a Swiss—a man we know nothing of—and you came to find the whereabouts of Bastineau."

"But I don't ask for so much as a glimpse of his face!" said Fenton. "I have my work. It is in Lyon to be done, and I'm going back to do it. But first I want to know from you that he's alive somewhere, climbing the mountains still——"

"But that is all the secret police, the enemy agents, the gendarmes themselves ask to know of him!" cried Jeanne-Marie in the same low, passionate voice. "My father has been taken away so that they can break every bone in his body for what they can get from him about Bastineau! And you stand there like a spoiled child, stamping its foot for candy in a place where murder is being done!" Her voice broke now, and she jumped to her feet and held to the back of her chair as if for strength for a moment. "You have come back looking for him, perhaps for none of the reasons that the others are. Perhaps looking for him because of love," she said. "But what is love any more, one woman's love, and what is friendship? What is the feeling one has for one's own people—one's father, mother, even—in the face of these more desperate things? You can't have wine this year, and you can't have cake, and you can't have chocolate soufflé, Fenton! You'll have to do without them as we others have." For a moment it seemed she might step forward and lay her cheek in tender grief against the other girl's cheek, but still she did not move. "I haven't forgotten the words you used to speak at the chalet door before you went out or before you went in—the charm

102

to make the dessert right, or the snow right for skiing! But this year there aren't any charms to say, and even friendship has to go through fire. And love—you'll have to do what the other women in this world are doing, Fenton. You'll have to put love aside this year," she said.

"I am not a child any more," said Fenton. "I have driven week after week from one town to another since I have been back in France. I have weighed school children—French school children—by the hundreds, and I have seen them gain, little by little, so heartbreakingly little, every week because of that pitiful handful of dried vegetables that we are able to give. I have seen students unable to pass their examinations because of hunger—actual hunger. I have grown up a little," she said. "I know that children who should gain seven centimeters in height every year are now gaining less than half of that. I have learned this is occupation! It isn't only German soldiers strutting down a street. It is these things that no generation to come can ever make up for. I have seen this, and I have earned in some part a right to share in France's fate——"

A low knock on the door interrupted her now, and Jeanne-Marie dropped her hand for silence on her arm.

"Wait," she said, and she crossed quickly to the other end of the room, and she turned the key in the lock, and drew back the iron chain. When she opened it partially, she stepped back a little, and a man in a corduroy working suit slipped quietly in.

He stood in the kitchen, looking from one to the other of them, as Jeanne-Marie bolted the door again—a stocky, heavily mustached man who had taken off his beaked cap respectfully before them and stood holding it in his hand.

"Where are you from?" said Jeanne-Marie quickly to him.

"From Lyon, *mademoiselle*," he said in a low voice. "I got through in the vegetable lorry. The *service* slipped me on at the wholesale market quays."

"Has anyone seen you come?" asked Jeanne-Marie.

"I kept to the back streets. I passed no one," he said. Then he took the Norwegian mittens from the pocket of his coat. "I'm a stranger in the mountains," he said, and he handed the pair of mittens to her. "I found the way here by the pattern, the way it was explained to me," he said.

Jeanne-Marie opened the kitchen-table drawer, and she dropped the pair of mittens in. Then she took a bottle of cognac from the shelf, and she motioned him to a chair.

"Tell me—have you news of my father?" she said. And at once, as if ashamed of this betrayal of herself, she poured the drink steadily for him and watched him lift the little glass. When he had drunk, he wiped his mustaches with the back of his hand.

"They shot fifteen in the prison courtyard yesterday morning," he said.

The color went from Jeanne-Marie's lips, and she laid one hand for strength upon the table. Fenton moved forward as if to put her arm about her, but she motioned her away.

"And you?" she said to the man seated at the table, and her voice was steady.

"Conscripted for labor in Germany. I'm not having any. I cleared out," he said.

104

"So you'll go higher, then?" asked Jeanne-Marie, and the question seemed to have meaning for him.

"Yes," he said. "That's what I came to do."

"You'll wait here out of sight until nightfall. There may be others," she said. She poured him another two fingers of drink. "And conditions in Lyon? Is there any trouble?" she said.

He sat looking a moment at the glass of cognac before him before he spoke.

"I saw a *bagarre* in the Lyon station yesterday," he said. "A trainload of prisoners returned by the Boches in exchange for conscripts to Germany." He took a quick swallow of the drink. "Here was the train of prisoners coming home on one track, and the *relevés* going out on the other. It was something to see," he said, and he smiled beneath his mustaches. "The prisoners were sick-enough-looking men, after three years of prison camp, but they could fight still. They jumped out onto the platform when they saw the train of conscripts, and they threw whatever they could lay their hands on— stones, benches, crowbars, baggage carts! They smashed the windows and broke the doors of that train of conscripts going out—Frenchmen accepting to go," he said, and he turned aside and spat onto the stove. "The prisoners shouted that they'd have stayed in prison where they were if they'd known that *relevés* were going out to work in factories in exchange. '*À bas* Laval!' you could hear the returned prisoners shouting, and the people took it up in the streets. It warmed your blood," he said.

"Yes," said Jeanne-Marie in a low voice. "Even the blood

that lies cold on the prison courtyards!" She stopped herself short then, and she turned and looked at Fenton. "Perhaps you had better go," she said. "There is no need to stay."

"If I can be of no help to you, I will go," said Fenton, and she stood fastening her coat over, buckling the belt in tight, drawing her gloves over her hands. They went out into the long, cold hall together, and at the front door Fenton turned and looked at Jeanne-Marie. "Will you tell me the truth about Bastineau now?" she said.

Jeanne-Marie waited a moment.

"If I tell you, will you say nothing and go back to Lyon in silence?" she said at last. "Will you see that the Swiss leaves Truex too?"

"Yes," said Fenton, and still she waited.

"Will you give me the note that Bastineau wrote so that I may destroy it?" said Jeanne-Marie. "No proof must remain that he is alive. Will you do that?" she said, her voice clear and low.

"Yes," said Fenton again, and Jeanne-Marie looked quickly about them.

"He is alive," she said, scarcely aloud. "He is alive, Fenton. He and Jacqueminot and the others are working on the frontiers."

"Working?" repeated Fenton.

"Contraband," said Jeanne-Marie in a scarcely audible voice. "Foodstuffs—woolens. The authorities do not know who is organizing this. They must not know."

"You mean—your father was willing to give his life for

this—for the black market?" Fenton said, and then she shook her head with impatience. "You ask me to believe that your father kept silent to protect a smuggling game?" She stood with her hands in the pockets of her coat, her hair flung back on her shoulders. "You expect me to believe this, Jeanne-Marie?" she asked incredulously.

"You promised that you would go—leave Truex, take the Swiss with you," said Jeanne-Marie in a quick, low voice. "Fenton, de Vaudois must not stay here. For the sake of these men on the frontier, will you keep that promise and see that he goes?"

"But de Vaudois is here on legitimate business," said Fenton impatiently.

"Ah, everyone comes on legitimate business—the secret agents first of all!" cried Jeanne-Marie, and then her voice broke. "Fenton, my poor friend, can't you see there is no reason for you to stay here now? Can't you see it the way it is?"

"I see that you will not tell me the truth," said Fenton bitterly.

"The truth is this," said Jeanne-Marie, speaking hurriedly to her. "I had hoped you would hear it from others—it is not easy for me to tell you this," she said, and she dropped her eyes. "Bastineau and I—we are to be married. It happened two years ago—we knew then we loved each other." Her fingers moved, trembling a little, to the brooch at her throat with the hunting horn of the Alpine Infantry curved on it. "You see, no matter how much you care, there is nothing for you to stay here for," she said.

Because of the bitterness of the thing of which they spoke, they had not seen the curé mount the stone steps from the street. But now he stood beside them, and his face was grave.

"Jeanne-Marie," he said quietly, and they saw the marks of grief set deep around his mouth.

For an instant, Jeanne-Marie seemed to falter, and then she raised her head and met his eyes.

"Yesterday?" she asked, scarcely aloud.

"Yes," said the curé gently. "They have sent me word in the customary way—that you may call for Jean-Pierre Favret's clothes at the Lyon prison. That is all."

"Jeanne-Marie, Jeanne-Marie!" cried Fenton softly, in compassion. She did not say any more before she went down the steps from them in the cold of the morning, but she took Bastineau's note from her pocket, and she thrust it quickly, blindly, into Jeanne-Marie's hand.

Four

THE SNOW had begun to fall again as Fenton walked through the village streets to the hotel. It fell softly and steadily on the air, and the mountains were blotted from sight now, and even the village houses she passed were masked by the quietly dropping petals of snow. Her hands were cold, in spite of the gloves, and the blood moved slow and cold in her heart, and as she crossed the church square she looked up at the clock's face in the tower. It marked noon, she saw through the falling curtains of white, and the train for the valley would leave at three. *I have time to change, and pack, and go down on it.*

And tonight the long ride again, she thought; *the halts at scarcely lit stations, with no hope in the heart this time for what is to come, and the lonely streets of Lyon at dawn, with the Feldgrau uniforms standing on sentry duty at the hotel doors.*

Fenton saw Madame Perrin at once when she stopped at the café door to brush the fresh snow from her shoulders, and shake the handkerchief from her head. Madame Perrin was sitting on the leather-cushioned banquette against the café's farthest wall, the rouge high on her plump, mottled cheeks, and a glass of Campari on the table before her. A cigarette was in her fingers, and she was smiling as foolishly as a girl at de Vaudois opposite her at the table, his back turned to the empty café.

"*Tiens,* Mademoiselle Ravel!" Madame Perrin called out. Behind her, the wall mirror reflected in black, corrugated glory the waves of her retouched and handsomely set hair. "We were going to get a search party out after you!" she said, and de Vaudois looked into the mirror and raised his glass to Fenton. "Out all night!" said Madame Perrin playfully.

"Come and have a drink," said de Vaudois, turning on his chair. "You owe it to us after having made our hair turn gray."

"Ha, ha," laughed Madame Perrin, but she looked sharply at his face, and one hand stole quickly to her *coiffure.* "Perhaps she should rest a little after such a night out in the storm," she said, and her eyes moved black and hard and curious on Fenton's weary face.

"I'll sit with you a minute," said Fenton in sudden decision. *Will you keep your promise?* Jeanne-Marie's voice asked softly of her. *Will you leave Truex and take de Vaudois with you? For the sake of Bastineau and the other men on the frontiers, will you see to it that he goes?*

De Vaudois had stood up now, his coat held around his shoulders, and Fenton moved in past him and sat on the banquette.

"Would *madame* be good enough to serve us three Camparis?" he said.

"Ah, never a quarter of an hour off my feet!" said Madame Perrin, and her mouth was set in displeasure as she looked at Fenton. She raised herself, sighing, from the table, and her hips spread broad below the purple sweater as she walked on her stilted heels to the bar and took the three fresh glasses down.

"I would like a cigarette, *monsieur*," said Fenton then, and there was nothing but gentleness in her voice.

"I have waited three days for you to ask for one," said de Vaudois, and he smiled with a little show of triumph as he took the box from his pocket and opened the cardboard lid. Fenton took one purple-tipped, delicate cigarette from the others, and as he held the lighter to it, she watched the white scar on his cheek with careful eyes. The end of his mouth twitched slightly where it drew.

"What luck on the Mont Maudit?" she said.

"The storm drove us down." He watched her take the first breath in. "I wasn't sorry to come back, between ourselves," he said, and he lowered his voice as he said it to her now. "I didn't quite like the manner of the guides. The remarks they made among themselves, their way of roping me —not in the center but at the end." He looked at her over his glass, and he shrugged his heavy shoulders beneath his coat. "A sense of menace," he said. And then he heard Madame Perrin's step behind him, and he spoke casually again. "We got down last night, quite early. We waited dinner an hour for you," he said.

Madame Perrin came back to the table now, and she put the tray down with the three glasses on it, and she took her seat on the cushioned bench again and looked at Fenton's hair.

"Your ends need redoing," she said, and she touched her own hard, ebony curls with her fingers.

"Madame Perrin and I were talking about the legend of the mittens when you came in," de Vaudois said.

"Oh, the mittens!" said Madame Perrin. "Mademoiselle Ravel should be able to tell us about them! She was knitting them all day yesterday."

De Vaudois took a swallow of the Campari, and his small, quick eyes looked from one to the other of the women.

"Parallels in history are interesting to note. The women of France have knitted before," he said.

"The peasants have always knitted," said Fenton, smoking.

"Not when wool was not on sale to honest people," de Vaudois said. "But it is the legendary side of it I was referring to. I was using the parable of two brothers—two young men who failed to understand each other in a world where

112

understanding could have changed the course of history," he said.

"Ah, it sometimes happens like that in families," said Madame Perrin, sighing. Fenton watched her take a drink of the Campari. *She is thinking about the quarrel with Cousin Perrin,* she thought. *It has been on her mind since 1932.* "There are times when one's own family even——" said Madame Perrin as she sipped the Campari with elegance from her lifted glass.

"You mean, when you sold Cousin Perrin the goat?" said Fenton, smoking.

"Gustav paid a good price for it," said Madame Perrin in quick defense. "He bought it at La Roche at the fair. I had no place for it here in the town, so I sold it half price to Cousin Perrin. Half price because he was Gustav's brother! A lot of thanks I got for it," she said.

"But only half of the goat was Gustav's," said Fenton.

"Ah, that was Cousin Perrin's story!" Madame Perrin said.

De Vaudois' fingers drummed quickly, impatiently on the table as they talked. *If we keep him from speaking for a little,* thought Fenton, *he will say the more hotly what he has to say.*

"But the truth was that the goat couldn't be taken up the mountain to Cousin Perrin's farm," said Fenton. "Not even after Cousin Perrin had paid his money for it."

"Oh, you can't trust a peasant's word," said Madame Perrin.

"But only half of the goat was yours to sell," said Fenton.

113

"I remember the talk of it all the years when I was young. On the way home from the fair at La Roche, Gustav had given half of the goat to Dizot to settle a debt with him."

"It was one man's word against another's," said Madame Perrin.

"But you kept the goat, and you kept Cousin Perrin's money, too," said Fenton. "I remember my father arguing it out with you," she said.

"Because Cousin Perrin would never agree to pay Dizot for the other half," said Madame Perrin in annoyance now, and Fenton leaned back on the leather banquette and laughed and shook her head.

"Whatever differences people have," de Vaudois broke in, "can be magnified out of all proportion by partisans of either side. The brothers I was speaking of are cases in point. One boy was an honest, upright lad, and the other one was suspect. But the public split—as usual—into two camps, and so the fight was on."

"Ah, the public!" said Madame Perrin, sighing over her glass.

"Now, the honest young man of my story," said de Vaudois, "went up a mountain one summer day."

"Alone?" asked Fenton, and she took another cigarette from the box by de Vaudois' hand.

"With a guide," said de Vaudois, and he leaned forward to light it for her. "In the course of the climb," he said as he snapped his lighter closed, "the boy met with disaster."

"And the guide?" said Fenton, smoking quietly.

"I am convinced that the boy alone was killed," said de

114

Vaudois. He took another swallow of the drink. "But, of course, there were various stories spread."

"I heard it said time and again that the guide didn't fall with the avalanche," Madame Perrin said wisely then. "Right away in August they began saying that the guide freed himself by cutting the rope and that only the Swiss boy fell."

"I wasn't speaking of August," said de Vaudois, "or of any particular time and place. This is simply a legendary tale about two brothers, and how one of them died!"

"And the other one?" asked Fenton, smoking.

"Ah, the other one!" said de Vaudois, looking at his drink. "The other one had a singular occupation. He was interested in wool. He used to make trips to the valley to get hold of it, and he'd have it knitted into mittens for the trade."

"Ask Mademoiselle Ravel about that!" said Madame Perrin coyly.

"But *mademoiselle* doesn't come into the story!" said de Vaudois. "This is merely a parable about a family quarrel," he said. "The group of people on the side of the honest young man who had met disaster in the avalanche wanted to avenge him. Their opponents formed a sort of secret society, the insignia of which was the Norwegian mitten on the hand. And here is the singular part of it," said de Vaudois, and he looked at Fenton. "Peasant women would sit hour after hour, day and night, knitting mittens, with apparently no idea of why they did it! Whether for evil or for good, they simply didn't know. The only thing that is clear in the story is," he said, and he took a cigarette from the box, "that the brother who was killed was apparently attempting—as an honest man would in a country where clothing is as hard come by as food —to find out whom these elaborately made articles were destined for."

"Why do you call them brothers?" asked Fenton, smoking still.

"They belonged to the brotherhood of man," said de Vaudois, "and they should have lived in peace together. But when corruption and treachery are uppermost in a man or a race, then it is time for simple and honorable men to speak aloud. That boy was killed," he said, and he brought his open hand down hard upon the table. "He was deliberately killed," he said, and the scar stood white as chalk across his face.

"I liked him when he stopped here at the hotel. I always like the Swiss," said Madame Perrin, and her eyes seemed to look not on de Vaudois alone, but on the entire nation of them respecting order and respecting law. "I've never had a moment's trouble with any Swiss in the twenty years I've been in the hotel business," she said. "They pay their bills on time, and clean! I'd rather have fifty Swiss in my rooms than a hundred guests of any other nationality! The furniture never scratched, the rugs never soiled, never late for a meal, everything going like clockwork."

"Thank you, *madame*," said de Vaudois, clipping the words on his tongue.

Fenton glanced up at the clock above the bar, and then she looked at de Vaudois.

"I'm taking the afternoon train down," she said, and de Vaudois' eyes were in sudden question on her face.

"You're leaving?" he said. And *This is honest, this surprise,* thought Fenton. *He is trying to put it together, the reasons that have made me give up the thing I came here for and go.* "They've defeated you so soon?" he said, a little bitterly, and Fenton shrugged her shoulders.

"The weather's bad. The place is cold," she said. She looked at him across the table. "Why don't you give it up for the season?" she said. "The spring thaws will make it far easier than now."

"No," said de Vaudois. "My work here has just begun."

"So you're leaving us?" said Madame Perrin. She smiled at Fenton, and the blunt, varnished finger tips of one perpetually soiled and faded hand touched the black waves of her hair. "I suppose you'd like some lunch before you go?" she said. "Just give me two meat tickets and a bread ticket— I'll ask for only one bread ticket as long as it's your last meal with us." She got up from the table and crossed the room, and from the kitchen she called out: "If you would be kind enough to get the two meat tickets and the bread ticket for me now, *mademoiselle,* so that I'll have them before I start——"

"They're in my room," said Fenton. She pushed aside the glass she had not touched yet, and she stood up, weary still, to go. She heard the iron rounds being shifted on the kitchen stove as Madame Perrin dropped the fresh wood in, and she would have moved past de Vaudois' chair, except that now he spoke her name. He spoke in a low and urgent voice to her, and he did not lift his eyes from the red of the Campari that stained the bottom of his glass.

117

"In the name of God," he said, and the words were spoken in English to her. "In the name of God, do not leave Truex without me," he said.

Fenton had stopped short by the table at the sound of it, and now she waited. *Do not leave Truex without me*, the silence repeated, saying it swiftly, furtively from every corner now that he had ceased to speak. *Do not leave Truex without me*, it spread in quick, hushed terror through the café room, and Fenton's heart halted in mistrust and wonder an instant at the note of desperation that was there.

"What are you afraid of? What have you to fear?" she asked in a quiet voice, looking down, and still he did not lift his eyes.

"I am menaced. I feel it," he said. If one had not stood close to him, watching, one would not have seen his lips move or known that he was speaking at all. "You and I, we are foreigners," he said. "We have an obligation to each other. Whatever it is they want to do to us, let's not give them the chance of getting one of us alone." The scar twitched white in his cheek, and he looked down into the glass that stood before him on the table. "Once the storm is over, I'll go up again. Wait thirty-six, forty-eight hours," he said. "Then I'll be ready to go."

Madame Perrin stood in the kitchen doorway now, her hands on her hips below the purple sweater, her eyes in hard, bright misgiving on Fenton standing by his chair.

"The ration tickets?" she said, and she lifted one hand and rubbed the thumb and forefinger together, and de Vaudois faced suddenly about.

"I gave you three ration cards intact last night," he said, his voice short, peremptory. "Take the tickets from one of them." Madame Perrin did not move for a moment, and she did not speak, but she stood in the kitchen doorway, looking at Fenton bitterly. "Sit down," said de Vaudois in English, speaking quietly again, and Fenton turned to the banquette behind her, and sat down upon the leather of its seat. "Bring *mademoiselle* a drink she can drink," said de Vaudois shortly, and he did not turn his head to Madame Perrin.

"Cognac and water," said Fenton.

"It's not permitted today," said Madame Perrin in triumph from the kitchen door.

De Vaudois brought his hand down hard, and the glasses shook on the table.

"Bring her cognac and water, in the name of God!" he said. He did not speak again until it was on the table before her, and then he said shortly: "Cook her a meal. She's faint for want of food. Drink, *mademoiselle*," he said when Madame Perrin was in the kitchen again. "You need it badly," he said.

Fenton took the first swallow of the cognac.

"What is it I am to stay here and protect you from?" she asked in irony.

"It is this," said de Vaudois, speaking English still. "They have killed one man. They will not hesitate to kill another. If I go up the mountain alone with them, it would be playing into their hands. There would be no deterrent—no witness even—to what they may intend to do. I saw their eyes as we crossed the glacier yesterday. They have no love for me," he

119

said. He looked up now, and faced her over the glasses on the table. "I'm here alone, a Swiss. I'd like another neutral present. When the storm is over, I shall have one more try. I'm asking you, *mademoiselle*, to go up the mountain with me when I go."

"And if you go down in an avalanche as the Swiss boy did?" asked Fenton.

He shrugged his shoulders.

"I would give you my sister's address in Geneva before we set out," he said. "She is all of my family that is left. We have always been close to each other. If anything happens, I would like you to write to her——"

"And if nothing happens," said Fenton, "you will leave Truex when I go?"

He looked sharply across the table at her, and his voice was low when he spoke.

"Is it a bargain?" he said.

Fenton took another drink of the cognac. And *Fenton*, said Jeanne-Marie's voice in the silence, *de Vaudois must not stay here. Will you keep your promise and see that he goes?*

"A bargain if I had any climbing boots to wear," said Fenton. "Mine are worn through," she said, and she thrust one foot from under the table. He looked down at the broken side of it, and the sole that was falling away.

"You have friends here. You could borrow a pair from Mademoiselle Favret, for instance," he said.

"Ah, no," said Fenton, too quickly, and at the sound of it de Vaudois glanced up at her as if in surprise.

"Then the visit this morning—a bit of a fiasco?" he said.

"The visit?" repeated Fenton, and she looked up from her glass.

"Things might be simpler if we spoke frankly to each other," said de Vaudois, saying it in English still. "I saw you go in." He paused a moment. "I didn't like the look of the man in the corduroy suit who joined you later," he said.

That day and night the storm blew hard, and the following day the wind was still not spent. De Vaudois spread out maps of the mountain region on the desk in the hotel's office, and there he worked in silence, smoking the delicate cigarettes, and making notes on the heights of the peaks, the glaciers, the ravines, in his neat, methodical hand.

"Each to his calling," said Madame Perrin when Fenton would have dried the dishes for her in the afternoon. The wind cried outside in the street, and the clock struck out above the bar. "Put your finger in everyone else's business and ruin the hotel trade by tales about a goat," she said, and she walked on the incongruous heels from stove to sink, from sink to stove. "Charm the men while you can, for later it won't be easy. It's dark women you read of in history. Blonde skin wrinkles too quickly. It dries up like crepe," she said as she slammed the saucepans down.

"Blonde women keep their tempers," said Fenton. She sat by the window, watching the snow blow hard across the glass.

On the wall, a calendar hung, with the day and the month marked boldly on it. *Le Deux Novembre*, it said, the letters of it in separate strokes like seconds ticking the substance of time away. *Only four days have passed since I came,* thought Fenton, and the clock struck four in the café. *Hour by hour, the day and the week, the time of waiting, the indecision are moving to their appointed end.*

"Only four days have passed since I came," she said aloud in the kitchen.

"And you're already eight hundred grams of bread tickets short," said Madame Perrin bitterly.

In the late afternoon, Fenton pulled the waterproof jacket over her head in impatience, tied the hood of it at her throat, and went out through the wildly blowing streets to the guides' café. The place was crowded and loud with voices, and the wind from the open doorway stirred the pipe smoke hanging on the air. Here were Virgil and Dizot, and beyond was Marc, and here and there at the tables she passed were the faces of guides she knew. There was Falcroz, the grizzled hair, and the falcon's nose beneath the hat, and *"Bon soir!"* he called out to her as she passed, and *"Bon soir!"* she called out in answer, but nowhere among the others was the face of Jacqueminot. She crossed quickly to the kitchen door, and there old Chatelard stood heating the *café nationale* on the stove, his carpenter's apron knotted on him, his hair pure white and silky beneath the light.

"Is Jacqueminot back?" she said in a low voice to him. "Did he get down through the storm?"

"There are times when he's gone a week and more," the old man said, and he shifted the saucepan on the flame.

"But the blizzard——" said Fenton.

"An early blizzard passes fast," old Chatelard said. "The snow of it goes overnight. They are safe in the mountains where they are."

He turned to the table now and fumbled for the cups, and Fenton put them into his hands.

"There are many of them, many more than their names can be told," he said. "Strong men, good men, and more of them coming. The passes belong to them, the torrents, the avalanches. You need not fear for Jacqueminot and the others. They can hold out against any army the Boches send. They can set the side of a mountain sliding if they only lift their hands."

"Jacqueminot and the others," repeated Fenton. And then she said: "Père Chatelard, when the weather settles, I shall be going with the Swiss' party up to the avalanche."

"It is not wise for foreigners to climb too high," said the old man gently, and he lifted the saucepan of coffee and slowly poured the cups full to the brim.

"Not even to look for the dead?" asked Fenton.

"He is not looking for the dead. He seeks the living," said old Chatelard. "Do not go. Do not ask to share the fate the mountains hold for him." His veined ancient hand took the cups from the stove now and set them on the tray before her. "Take the coffee in to the men," he said, "while I rake the ashes down."

When Fenton came back, he was standing by the fire still, and he looked at her with tenderness through his dim, faded eyes.

"There was something from a long time back," he said,

123

and his mind groped for it, touched this year and that, seeking the words of it, and the hour, the place, the day. "The first night you came in with the Swiss, it was here," he said, and his thick, gnarled fingers tapped slowly on his heart.

"Was it something—something to do with Bastineau?" she said, but even as she spoke his name, she felt the shame hot in her. *He has nothing to do with you any more*, she thought in quick rebuke. *He belongs to a prouder woman. He belongs to a woman of silence and fortitude, while you stand here in weakness, crying out his name.*

"Bastineau," the old man said. "He never came in here with a woman after. He'd come in in the evening and sit down at the table where you sat, and not at any other table. There's a mark on the wood, cut in the table's corner by the wall," he said, and he groped now for the cups. "He carved it there one evening while he sang."

"But he went to war," said Fenton, and her voice was soft. "He couldn't have come in."

"There were Saturday nights when they'd come down from the frontier," old Chatelard said. "They'd sit at that same table where you sat, he and Jacqueminot together, or sometimes Bastineau alone. Maybe he had a photograph of you," he said.

"A photograph?" said Fenton, scarcely aloud.

"It might have been you," the old man said, but the sense of it was going dim. "A little girl, fifteen or sixteen it might be, with her hair in braids." He filled the cups slowly with the coffee again. "Come into the café and you'll see the sign he cut there in the table," he said, and Fenton took two of the steaming cups from the stove and followed him through the door.

The wind had fallen now as she went through the snowy streets alone, and her heart was no longer numb within her, for the shape of what Bastineau had carved in the table's wood stood strong and perfect before her in the dark. She took the way across the bridge, and it was sight and sound and breath in her nostrils, it was music playing in her ears. It shone in the light of the street lamps she passed, it gleamed before her like a bright, indelible crown marvelously fallen on every step of snow. The sky was clearing overhead, and the stars repeated it in high and icy promise. The reflection of it stood in every darkened window on the square. It was there in the mirror of her hotel room when she stood before it—not her own face, or the light hair falling on her shoulders, but the letters he had carved in the table's wood etched brilliantly forever on the glass. She could see the small, exactly shaped circle of it, and once you had read the words, you read them again in rotation, as if they were written upon a turning wheel. *Ci-gît mon coeur*, it was carved in the shape of a ring slipped on the finger: *Here*, he had written, *on the corner of this table lies, deep in the wood and as uncorruptible, my heart.*

She wore it down to supper like a bracelet of diamonds on her wrist, like pearls in her ears, like a crown of delicate flowers laid upon her hair. *Ci-gît mon coeur*, said the food that seemed suddenly lavish on the table before her, and the watered wine in her glass was strong and fragrant as it had

125

never been before. The look of accusation in Jeanne-Marie's eyes was gone now, and Jeanne-Marie's voice was silent. There was no curved hunting horn on the brooch at her throat, and if she sought to speak in protest, the words were not said loud enough for Fenton to hear. *He carved it in wood,* the joy cried out in Fenton's veins. *He set it there like a landmark so that I would always find the way! Ci-gît mon coeur,* said the pulse at her wrist, and she watched it beating, like the heart of a captured bird. The questions, the misgivings had not begun yet; they stood in the darkness and sleeplessness, waiting. *Things have altered since he carved that in the table while he sang,* she did not let the bitter silence say.

She had finished the *potage national,* and it was while she ate the plate of lentils that de Vaudois came in through the café door. He crossed the room, making his way among the empty tables, and he pulled out the chair and sat down facing her. He took the neat little perfumed box of cigarettes from his pocket, and he held them out to her across the cloth.

"I have found you a pair of mountain boots. New ones," he said, and he smiled as he held the flame of the lighter for her. "Falcroz says the indications for good weather are excellent. We shall be setting off before dawn."

"I shall be ready," Fenton said.

It was the morning of November the third when they set out, and it was dark still as they mounted toward the glaciers through the trees. The guides had their ropes coiled at their waists, the loaded rucksacks on their backs, and there was little speech among them as they climbed. Because of the freshly fallen snow, the going was hard, and they took it slowly:

126

Falcroz ahead, breaking the way through the forest for them, and the younger guides alternating with him, while Fenton and de Vaudois walked singly and in silence, hour after long, slogging hour, behind. When the first wash of light came gray through the trees, and the shape of the moving men came clear before them, Fenton saw the thing that one guide bore lashed to his pack, and her heart went cold an instant. It hung stiff as a corpse's arm across his neck—the canvas in which the living enshrouded and bore down across the ice the mountain dead. *They have killed one man. They will not hesitate to kill another,* said the echo of de Vaudois' voice, and she heard Père Chatelard say it in warning to her: *Do not go,* he said; *do not ask to share the fate the mountains hold for him.*

By one o'clock in the day, they had reached the rocks of Trélaporte, and they made the break there, stopping on the islands of stone in the hot, bright sun. They slipped their packs from their shoulders, and they sat down to rest and to eat their rations of bread and cheese on the edge of the pure white, glacial world.

"It isn't the time of year for climbing high," said one guide among them, and he looked out across the rising highways of ice.

"In November excursionists stay home. Only the military need to bivouac," another guide went on with the complaint, and de Vaudois turned sharply on them.

"The fee looked just as good to you in November as it did in August, didn't it?" he said.

The guide with the pipe between his teeth considered it for a moment.

127

"Better," he said then, and the others laughed aloud.

"Men can make it in any month," said Falcroz, breaking his dry bread. "But it isn't a climb for a woman."

"This isn't a pleasure trip," said de Vaudois, clipping the words short. "You're being well paid for what you're asked to do."

They sat eating in quiet a little while in the bright, clear air, and then Falcroz looked up to the heights before them, and he spoke of the Col des Hirondelles, where the swallows passed over in the autumn and spring.

"They'll pass over there by the hundreds in the right months," he said, and with his weathered hand he traced the curve before them. "They'll take that way across as if there weren't another pass on the range," he said, "migrating from north to south, or south to north, depending on the season——"

"Because it's lower—more accessible?" de Vaudois asked, and his voice was sharp.

"Ah, not being a swallow, I wouldn't know the reason," Falcroz said in his slow, patient, mountain speech, and the other guides threw back their heads and laughed across the snow.

"Is the Col des Hirondelles that gap over there?" de Vaudois persisted. "Is that it—directly before us—east, I should say?" And now he reached for his rucksack on the rock beside him, and he unbuckled one pocket of it, and Fenton saw him take the pair of binoculars out. He got to his feet behind the other men, and he stood erect a moment on the rock, the

128

glasses lifted, his eyes searching beyond the glaciers to the ridge which marked the frontier in the eternal snows.

But now Falcroz turned his head, and he saw that de Vaudois was standing and that he held binoculars to his eyes.

"Ah, that you're not permitted!" the old guide cried out, and he stumbled to his feet. Under the felt hat's brim, the blood stood red in his weathered cheeks, and his nose and his chin jutted sharp and hard as stone. "You signed a paper in the *gendarmerie* below. No cameras, no field glasses. You're in a military zone," he said.

De Vaudois lowered the binoculars while Falcroz spoke, and he looked at him, the eye cold, contemptuous, the mouth twitching to the white seam of the scar.

"I pay for what I want," de Vaudois said, and he moved to lift the glasses to his eyes again, but the guide's hand quickly caught his wrist.

"Not for this," said Falcroz. "For this no living man can pay." He said it without anger, but his fingers were closed as implacable as steel upon the lifted arm; and it may have been this word or act or this look in Falcroz' eyes for which the others had been waiting, for now Fenton saw the four guides rise quietly, almost stealthily, from their places on the rocks and jump as quick as cats across the patches of fresh snow. "Give me the glasses peaceably and no harm will have been done," Falcroz said, and de Vaudois turned his head, and something as violent as the hand of death itself passed over and transformed his face when he saw the others standing, waiting, there.

"In every mountain expedition there is a *chef*," he began.

"Yes, there is a *chef*," said Falcroz, and he buckled the pair of binoculars into his pack. "There is a *chef*," he said, and he swung the rucksack onto his shoulders, and the others did as he did, and in single file again they followed where he led across the snow.

As they climbed higher in the afternoon, de Vaudois looked fearfully at times, it seemed to Fenton, down the perilous drop below the path to the icefall below. Three guides climbed before them, and two behind, and de Vaudois kept his eyes in apprehension on them. *Whatever it is they want to do to us*, said the nervousness of his fingers upon the ice ax he carried, *let's not give them the chance of getting one of us alone*. It was early still when they reached the Requin hut, but the sun had gone from the high, white, icy valley, and Falcroz called down from the rocks above that this was the end of the day.

"It's just after three," said de Vaudois under his breath, and he stopped in the path and looked at the watch on his wrist. "We can make the second refuge if we push on. I wanted to get farther——"

"We don't cross the *séracs* in the dark," said the guide behind him. "Not if we want to come back alive," he said, and de Vaudois climbed in silence the last steep spiral of the path.

The Requin hut stood high, built on the last red lip of rock, and on three sides of its shelf dropped the glacial falls of ice, shadowed and crevassed with premature evening now in bottle green and blue. Falcroz opened the cabin door with the key that hung there for passing mountaineers to use, and they stamped their feet free of snow at the entrance and followed him in from the silent breath of cold.

"We'll make the second hut by tomorrow noon," the old guide said as he swung his rucksack to the floor.

"And the avalanche?" asked de Vaudois, his eyes sharp on his face.

"The morning after that," said Falcroz. "The days are short now. The going is not easy in fresh snow." At supper he said again: "It is not a climb for a woman to take. We'd go faster if *mademoiselle* would wait for us here at the Requin."

"I can climb as well as a man," said Fenton, and she saw that de Vaudois' hand was unsteady as he put the glass of coffee down. And *If he fears to go on alone with them*, she thought, *then what power within him or beyond him insists that he must go? Or is this the part he is playing now so that I will not forsake him? He believes that I have come this far through pity, and that pity for him will take me the rest of the way.*

"You made the arrangements with me, Falcroz. You can stand by them now," de Vaudois said. *But why did he want me out of Truex?* thought Fenton, eating as the others ate. *Why did he want me where he could watch me night and day?* And old Chatelard's voice said gently to her: *He is not looking for the dead. He is seeking the living.* And then her heart seemed to halt an instant, shocked suddenly by recognition. *He is seeking the living*, she repeated. *Perhaps he believes that I will unwittingly show him the way.*

By seven they had cleaned the remains of food from the table, and the guides had smoked their final pipes, and unlaced their shoes and set them aside. The candles that stood in the wine-bottle mouths were extinguished between callused finger and thumb, and the men lay down on their bunks with their blankets around them, and turned their faces to the wall. They had taken one side of the refuge room, where the tiers of bunks stood, and left the other side to de Vaudois, where the single bunk was placed between the kitchen and the washroom door. Fenton would sleep in the little room beyond, said Falcroz, and before she went to her bunk there, he made a joke about the snoring of the guides.

"Leave the door open so as to share the heat of the fire with us," he said. "But if we snore too loud, I'll close it in the night."

She kept on her clothes for warmth, and she wrapped the coarse, soiled blanket around her, and spread her scarf on the ticking of the ancient pillow before settling it beneath her head. From where she lay, she could see the fire's light through the partially open door, and now de Vaudois began to pace up and down on the boards beyond, smoking cigarette after cigarette in the darkness, and casting the still unfinished ends away. When he halted by the stove, his face was lit by the fire's glow, and she saw the look marked on it. *I am afraid to lie down here and sleep,* the quiet said. *I am afraid to lie down unconscious here where the Swiss boy must have slept before he died.*

"We start at daybreak," Falcroz said at last from his bunk. "You would do better to stop the cigarettes now if you want to have breath for the climb———"

If I want to have breath for the climb! If I want to have breath, repeated the silence, and the scar slashed white across de Vaudois' face, and he passed his hand over his hair. *There's a man lying up there, without breath, in the snow*, said his eyes as he leaned above the stove's red arc of light. But he went to his bunk now, and lay down on it, and for the little while before she fell asleep, Fenton watched his hand hanging tense from the blanket's fold, and the fingers tapping steadily on the bare plank of the edge.

She remembered the noises of the night—the men calling out or moaning in their sleep, and the sound of the stove's irons being lifted as a guide stumbled over his boots in slumber to put the fresh wood in. But when she awoke in the early day, she saw they had closed the door while she slept, and in the cold, little room the ice was blooming in stiff-petaled flowers upon the windowpanes. She hugged herself in her arms in her flannel shirt for warmth, and she walked on wool-socked feet to the door and opened it, and there was the absolute silence of the refuge room. The bunks were empty, the shoes, the rucksacks, the men were gone, but the fire burned low still in the stove. She looked at the place in bewilderment a moment, and then she saw her own pack had been lifted to the table, with a bit of paper pinned high, as if in signal on the canvas of it, and she crossed the room, hugging herself in her arms still, and undid the paper with fingers gone clumsy in the cold. She stood by the fire for warmth, then, reading the penciled words.

133

Mademoiselle: Excuses for going on without you. It is not a trip for a woman this time of year. Monsieur did not wish to leave you, but we persuaded him among us. We would have left a guide to take you back to Truex, but we could not spare one from the work we have to do. Mademoiselle, you know the danger of the mountains and you will not try to descend the glacier alone. There is food enough and fuel in the kitchen. We will be back in two days, when we have finished,

and the old guide's signature, "Falcroz," stood with a flourish at the end.

Fenton folded the paper into her pocket, and put fresh wood in the stove, and then she opened the door of the refuge and stepped out into the cold of the early day. Before her, and below, in the high, white, cloudless dawn rose and descended the marble stairways, brittle and vast and seemingly impassable. *They would be going roped three by three*, she thought, and she slowly scanned the *séracs*, the towers, the glacial precipices up to the far unblemished névé that stood soft as velvet above the falls. *I would have made the uneven number. Another good mountaineering reason for them to have let me sleep*, she thought, and she stood on the rock before the hut, watching for movement among the horns of the *séracs*. *I should still be able to see them, moving there ahead*, she said to the arched, white, static dawn. *And now that they have de Vaudois, what will they do to him?* she thought, and her teeth chattered suddenly with the cold. *We persuaded him among us*, said the words of Falcroz' message, and she held herself in her arms to keep her bones from shaking, and something that may have been pity or may have been fear moved her as she stood watching for the two black threads of men weaving in and out of the falls.

But there was no shadow, no whisper of life in the frozen world before her, and she went into the refuge again and put more wood on the fire. The thought of food, of hot coffee, bread, came quickly to her then, and she went to the kitchen for a saucepan, and back to the refuge door again to fill it with snow. She had opened the door to step out, but instead she stood motionless on the threshold, for two men stood on the path before her. They carried ice axes on their shoulders, and crampons hung from their belts, and the shapeless hats of mountain men were pulled sideways on their heads. The first one was tall and lean, with an unshaven face and hollow cheeks, and he was a stranger to her. The other was Bastineau.

"Fenton, it's crazy. Fenton, *c'est fou*," he said, and they stood there in the early-morning light of what might have been spring or what might have been summer, looking without equivocation into each other's eyes.

She did not remember after if the sun rose that morning, or if snow fell, or if clouds or swallows moved over the passes, for the sound of his voice had altered the season forever. Whether she spoke then, or later, or what it was she said, she did not know. She backed into the room again as the two men crossed the step, and she watched them close the door, and sling down their packs, and she stood there, her two hands holding to the saucepan as if it alone were the shape and substance of reality. She stood by the stove with her eyes on his height and the breadth of his shoulders, on the sight of his face at last before her: the flesh and blood of Bastineau's face,

135

with the skin burned dark as leather, and the teeth bone-white, and the eyes unaltered, quick, black, and merry as a boy's.

"Bastineau, how are you? How are you?" she said, and her breath seemed to perish with it.

"I'm aging. I've got gray in my hair," he said, and he took off the worn felt hat and bent his head to show the short, black lively locks of it to her. "Fenton, you're sixteen still. How do you do it?" he said, and in a minute he might laugh aloud. He tossed his hat back on the table, and the medals on it sounded out as they struck the wood, and he did not take his eyes from Fenton. "Did we make the rendezvous here three years ago?" he said, and she saw him look quickly at her fingers on the handle of the saucepan still, as if to see if any ring were there. "I saw the smoke all the way down, and I didn't like it," he said. "So we crossed flat as eels. We were just below when you came out the first time and stood watching—— *Dieu!*" he said, breaking off, and he sprang suddenly across the room, his step quick, light, and looked into the kitchen, into the washroom, into the little room where Fenton had slept. "I didn't ask you if you were alone?" he said.

"Yes. The others went up before dawn," said Fenton, and she watched the thing go quiet in his face. When he came back, he stood so close that she felt his breath upon her hair.

"Then we can talk a bit while we eat," he said, and now, as if they had thought for the first time of him, they both looked toward the other man. "This is a friend," said Bastineau. "An Austrian. Like all outlaws, he has no name. He's come a long way, and he's going farther. His way and mine part here."

136

The stranger with the hollow cheeks bowed shyly to Fenton, and then he spoke in English to her.

"When we saw you from below, Bastineau said you were American," he said. His eyes, the whites of them bloodshot from fatigue, were diffident in his gaunt, young face, and his accent was clearly Oxford. "I must ask you to excuse my appearance this morning," he said, and he drew one hand self-consciously along his chin.

"A time to speak of beards in any language, with the Fascisti firing on you yesterday!" said Bastineau, and he threw his head back and laughed aloud. "But say it in French, if you have to," he said, "for that and patois are my language," and then he reached forward without warning and his quick, strong fingers took the saucepan from Fenton's hand. "Get the fire going well, *mes enfants*," he said. "I'll get the snow for the coffee." At the door, he turned and looked back at Fenton. "The food cache is under the bunk in the other room," he said. "We'll have a good meal together here before he goes down, for God knows when he'll get another. They don't issue ration cards to men who come in by the glaciers," he said.

While the snow melted in the saucepan on the fire, Bastineau ground the coffee, seated on the bench with the coffee mill held between his knees. The Austrian set the tin plates and cups on the table's boards, and Fenton sliced the wheel of country bread and the sausage. The side of ham was there, and the slab of cheese, and the butter even, and the Austrian's eyes were on them, hungrily.

"Last night I saw the first real bread I've seen in four

137

years," he said. "Up in the cabin at the pass, with Bastineau."

"We've been ten hours coming down," said Bastineau, and he tapped the little drawerful of ground coffee into the filter's top. "Fresh snow made it treacherous," he said, and now he was pouring the boiling water slowly through. "Lad's on his way to England," he said, and he jerked his chin at the Austrian. "Wants to see if they still play cricket. He went to school over there."

"I've been thinking a bit as we came down," the Austrian said, his eyes abashed again, and the color flushing his neck. "Perhaps my place isn't over there," he said. "Perhaps my place is here with you."

"Some go on, some join up with us," Bastineau said. The coffee was dripping in the pot on the corner of the three-legged stove, and he twisted the corkscrew into the bottle of wine. "The fight's the same, whichever it is," he said. "You've a chance of getting through." The cork came out, and he set the bottle on the table. "There're a lot of hungry men up there. You saw them," he said to the Austrian. "And food a little scarce," he said, and he swung one leg over the bench and sat down at the table.

"If I can get the information—the location through," the Austrian began, and then he stopped talking suddenly and looked across the table. "You haven't said anything. Perhaps I shouldn't talk here," he said.

"Go on," said Bastineau, and he wolfed the bread with the ham thick on it. Then he took a swallow of coffee to wash it down. "Go on. She's my child," he said. "I brought her up." He reached forward quickly across Fenton, and cut a slice of

138

cheese. "But once you're over the glacier, you say nothing at all. You pick up Jacqueminot at the Chapeau. From then on, you're quiet. Eat," he said, looking quickly at Fenton, and his cheek was full of bread.

"I can't eat," said Fenton. She sat with her arms in the flannel shirt folded on the table, her eyes fixed on him. "I can't do anything but look at you. They told me you were dead."

"I am," said Bastineau, chewing. "Dropped into a crevasse the first week of the armistice. Pass your hand through me. I'm spirit. I'm not flesh and blood."

"You're Bastineau," said Fenton, and she thought: *I like the way your hair grows, I like the way the muscles move in your temple when you eat.* "Dead or alive, it doesn't matter. You're absolutely Bastineau," she said.

"This child," said Bastineau to the Austrian, and he motioned toward her with his knife, "she used to get killed—or nearly—every season. Once I fished her out of a frog pond, and once I found her thrown from a horse on the road in the dark——"

"Oh, don't, don't, Bastineau!" Fenton cried out, and she felt the blood come into her face. *Don't tell him I was fifteen that year, and that I died of shame every time I remembered it after! Don't tell him there were arms in a jacket around me, and I couldn't stop the sound of my voice from saying: "Bastineau, I love you. I love you, Bastineau."*

"And once we were coming down fast and she took the drifts to the side instead of the tracks," he said.

"And he skied down, carrying me," she said in humiliation.

I like the way you're hungry and thirsty, she thought as she watched him. *I like the way you laugh out loud.*

"Bastineau's the protector," said the Austrian quietly, and his eyes were shy.

"We're not playing belote this year," said Bastineau. "The stakes are running higher." He swung his leg over the bench, and he reached for the pot of coffee on the stove. "I'm not in it alone," he said, and he filled the Austrian's cup first. "I didn't die because I saw another way out. Collaboration. Between outlaws, that is."

"He's the man we pray to in concentration camps on the other side of these mountains," the Austrian said, and his young eyes were on Fenton. "He's the word we whisper to one another in hope. He's promise to us—he and the other men like him. He's holding the last door open for us, holding it like this, when every other door has closed."

"Eat," said Bastineau, and he cut another piece of bread and passed it on the knife point to the Austrian. "He's been in Dachau. Stripes across his back," he said to Fenton, and he jerked his head toward the other man. "They broke his jaw for him. That didn't finish him," he said. "He got out, crossed into Italy. He lived like a rat in the sewers there, but he found the right men in the end. They passed him on. He made Courmayeur, where the *carabinieri* shot at him yesterday."

"Once the ascent through the woods began, I was under cover," the Austrian said as he ate.

"We can keep on getting men through until they change the Italian military on the other side of the Col," said Basti-

140

neau. "Lads from Mentone who were still French three years back. They had to take the oath of allegiance to the Duce—matter of form—but they're with us. We've got an army that can hold out if the supplies can get that high." He took another swallow of coffee. "Take some ham," he said to the Austrian. "You've got a stretch to do before you hit Marseille."

"But the business of contraband?" said Fenton, and she sat there watching him as if she could never see enough of his face.

"He's contraband," said Bastineau. He stood up to pour a glass of red wine for the other man, and his quick, strong hand fell on the Austrian's shoulder an instant. "He's contraband of war. There're hundreds like him. In Marseille he'll live in the sewers again, but he'll get out. He'll ship to Casablanca with false papers, because the *service* is behind him," he said.

"It may be a while," said the Austrian as if in apology, "but if I get through, I'll make them understand what's needed if it's the last thing I do."

"Arms and supplies, dropped by parachute, do you see, Fenton?" said Bastineau, and his face and his voice had altered. He looked quickly at the Austrian again. "We'll hold out," he said. "Partisans, saboteurs, fugitives from conscription, men out of prison camp, and from the Occupied—we're used to patience and pulling the belt a hole or two tighter. Once we get what is needed, they won't have to teach us how to fight," he said.

"Bastineau," said Fenton, and the food and the wine stood

untouched before her. "You say these things to me as if I were one of you. The others—Jacqueminot—Jeanne-Marie—they didn't——"

"Part of their business is to make the smokescreen. Mine's not," he said, and his hand dropped quick and strong upon her hand. "I'm not in it alone. There's Socquet, and Couttet, and Ravanel, and a hundred others. There's half the valley down there taking the food from its own mouth to carry it up to the Calvary. There's Cousin Perrin, and La Cousine; there's *monsieur le curé*; there's Jacqueminot and Jeanne-Marie." Fenton's breath stopped short for a moment, but his face had not altered as he spoke the name. "They don't want to sell our skins for us. Fenton," he said, speaking quickly still, "they didn't tell me you were back—none of them told me. They probably knew that if they had, I'd have chanced it and gone down."

She felt her hand tremble under his on the table's boards, and she could not look in his face now—and then the voice of Jeanne-Marie spoke in clear, high rebuke across the room. *We are to be married, Bastineau and I*, said Jeanne-Marie's voice, and Fenton drew her hand from under his hand. *I might be nothing but a child still*, she thought in sudden bitterness. *I might have pigtails hanging down my back still, and my skirts above my knees. He touches my hand as if it were a child's hand, and his promise of love is given to a woman. To him it is nothing to walk into a mountain refuge and find me, and to me it's the three years without him that have stopped crying their hearts out at last.*

"I haven't asked you any questions," said Bastineau, and

his eyes beneath his straight black brows were dark and quick. "Perhaps because I always thought it was going to happen this way."

"I was left behind by accident," said Fenton, and still she could not look into his face. "I gave my word to de Vaudois that I would go."

"That was the party going up toward the Vallée Blanche this morning. We saw them from behind the névé," Bastineau said, and he stood up from the table. "Jacqueminot said to watch for them when the weather cleared. We got past them safely. You'll have to be getting down," he said to the Austrian, and his voice and his gait as he walked toward the stove were as casual and lazy as a resting mountaineer's should be.

Fenton took the note from Falcroz out of the pocket of her flannel shirt, and she gave it to him. He stood by the stove, his dark head bent, and he read it through.

"Falcroz had his reasons for leaving you behind," he said. "If de Vaudois tries to see too much, there may be a bit of trouble."

"He was afraid of the guides," said Fenton. "Or he wanted me to believe it. He gave me his sister's address in Switzerland. If he doesn't come back, I'm to let her know——"

"I'll copy it down," said Bastineau. "We know the dead boy was an agent—Boche, not Swiss—sent up to smoke us out. The *service* had the data on him."

"But the avalanche that killed him in August?" Fenton said.

"Intentional," said Bastineau, and he leaned on the cor-

143

ner of the table, copying down the name, and the street, and the number in Geneva. "Falcroz took him across at the wrong hour," he said, straightening up. "He cut the rope and let him fall. He wouldn't have liked having to do that to you——"

"Falcroz—in cold blood——" said Fenton, and her heart was sick for a moment.

"Is the blood cold?" asked Bastineau, and now his eyes were sober on her face. "Let's say it's hot, loyal, furious blood instead, ready to kill a Swiss boy, a de Vaudois—to kill you even, Fenton. Loyal enough to close the eyes so as not to see your mouth or hair, and to cut the rope and set the avalanche going. Falcroz left you behind. It was because he saw what might have to come."

He was making ready to go now, and *Don't, ah, don't,* she cried out in silence. *There are three years of waiting to make up for! There are three years of hearing nothing at all because I did not hear you speak. I've seen only half of your face this time, and touched only one of your hands!* And *Shame, oh, shame,* said Jeanne-Marie in rebuke to her. *He has nothing to do with you now, this man called Bastineau.*

"Shall I pack food for you?" asked Fenton quickly.

"Not for me, for the Austrian," said Bastineau. "We'll have to be moving fast. You have the map?" he said to the other man, and as Fenton cut the bread and cheese on the table, the Austrian took the Norwegian mitten out.

Then he stood there a moment, feeling in his pockets.

"There's only one. I must have dropped the other coming over the *séracs,*" he said.

"That much wool lost," said Bastineau, "but the pattern's the same." He laid the mitten flat on the palm of his hand, and his forefinger, with the blackened nail on it, traced slowly along the markings in the wool. "Here is the Chapeau," he said, and his finger halted on the stag's head. "Jacqueminot is coming down the Glacier d'Argentière bringing the others through from Switzerland. Take it slowly. The spear points indicate the worst of the crevasses. They're covered, and they're treacherous." His finger traced the way on the mitten's back again. "The arrows indicate the points of the compass. The Chapeau is almost due north. Jacqueminot will be there by evening. Wait for him," he said.

The Austrian folded the mitten in his pocket again, and Fenton buckled his food in his rucksack's pouch.

"Thank you," he said. "I shan't forget what you've done."

"Ah, say it to Bastineau, not to me," said Fenton in a low voice.

"I say it to you," said the Austrian, and the color rose under his beard again, "because there are no words to say it to Bastineau."

"You've food enough here," said Bastineau quickly to her.

"Yes," she said, and she put more wood on the fire so as not to see him buttoning his jacket across.

"I've got a day's climb back," he said, and he hoisted his rucksack to his shoulders.

"Alone?" asked Fenton in sudden trepidation.

"Alone," he said, and his teeth were white in the bronzed skin of his face.

145

"If a snow bridge breaks?" said Fenton, and she could not take her eyes from him now.

"They'll hold for me," he said.

"They break for the best of guides," she said, and, scarcely knowing that she moved, she put out her hand and laid it on his arm.

"They'll hold for mountain men this year. The gods are with us," he said, and suddenly he dropped his head and kissed her fingers on his sleeve. "So you'll wait," he said. He stood straight now, and he pulled his hat on, and nothing had altered in his eyes. "If de Vaudois comes back, he's got to find you here." He undid the crampons from his belt, and he flattened the straps of them with his thumb. "You're in this now with the rest of us," he said. "You'll find out what he knows. You'll wipe our footsteps out of the snow up from the ice-fall, so there won't be any sign of us left. You'll stamp the tracks of the Austrian out once he's gone down. When he strikes the ice of the glacier, there'll be no trace, so you can leave it there." He stood before her, his eyes moving, quick, black, restless on her face. "He's your particular business now, de Vaudois," he said, and the sunlight fell bright across them, hot and sudden as fire, as he opened the refuge door. "This is the fourth," he said. "Let me know later what you've been able to get from him."

"But where?" said Fenton quickly. "When?" In a moment he might turn and be gone forever across the great wild sweeps of ice and snow.

He paused for a moment, the sunlight on his shoulders.

"The Montanvert," he said. "After nine at night, on the

eighth. You'll find the key on the window ledge, first window to the right of the front door."

"Yes," said Fenton, "yes," and she heard the exultant sound of it in her own voice. *So this isn't the end! I am to see him again!*—and she felt no sense of shame.

The Austrian stood before her in the doorway now, and Bastineau went out onto the pathway and, with his back to them, he waited there.

"Good going," said Fenton to the gaunt young man, and he shyly shook her hand.

"I'm glad for the accident that kept you here," he said, the abashed voice speaking English to her. "I shan't forget you" —saying it simply and without gallantry to her as he might have said: "I'm glad the sun came out today."

Then they were gone. They dropped out of sight below the rock, and she went to the edge to watch them, and she saw them shake each other's hands where the paths diverged below. Bastineau turned to the icefall on the right, and she lost him for a moment. When she saw him again, he was dwarfed by the distance, scarcely of human size any longer, leaping from rock to rock as he went down. In the other direction, going toward the glittering highways of the Mer de Glace, she could see the Austrian descending the trail which she and de Vaudois and the guides had marked in the drifts as they toiled upward. In another half-hour, the two dark, separately moving figures were lost from sight in the vastness of the glacial world.

It was not until she was back at the refuge door again that she saw the other thing—the pattern that had been traced

147

with the point of an ice ax, it may have been, lying diamond-sharp and brilliant in the snow. It was circular in shape, and the letters that formed it could be clearly read. *Ci-gît mon coeur*, it said, and Fenton kneeled quickly down and looked in wonder at it. *While the Austrian said good-by in the doorway, he wrote it then*, she thought, and she put her hands around its shape as tenderly as if it were the first bright, vulnerable crocuses of spring that had suddenly come to flower there.

All that morning she worked on the footsteps, filling them in or stamping them out: Bastineau's and the Austrian's steps up from the icefall, and Bastineau's alone descending the way again, and the footsteps that lay in confusion, some with the stamp of the peculiar nailheads deep in them, around the refuge door. But the circle of words she did not touch, and during the day, as the sun rose hot, the letters of it melted and altered until the sense itself had seemed to drip away. *I'll let it freeze here again tonight, and tomorrow I'll wipe it out. Tomorrow will be soon enough*, she thought, and sometimes in love, sometimes in shame, she returned to look at it and read its message there. And *Ah, Bastineau, Bastineau*, she said as she cut the bread alone at noon, *why must you do it to me still?* And Bastineau threw back his head in the sunlight and she heard him laugh aloud. *It doesn't mean anything, Fenton*, he said, and his teeth were white in his leathered face. *It simply is part of making life taste as wild as wine and as sweet as bread for a little, like singing loud when you're coming down fast through snow.*

When night came, she turned the key in the lock, and she

bolted the shutters at the window. *I am in it now,* she thought as she sought to fall asleep on the bunk in the little room. *I am in it the way Jeanne-Marie and the rest of them are. I am in it as the whole country is in it. Love for one man has nothing to do with it; it has got beyond that now. I shall go back to Lyon and serve this cause however they need me,* she thought, and the night passed slowly. *And love—you'll have to do what the other women in the world are doing,* said the darkness and loneliness of the refuge to her. *You'll have to put love aside this year.*

In the early morning, the flowers of ice bloomed on the windowpanes again, and the room was cold as she put the wood in on the glowing ash. *Then why does he mark the words of love like that?* she asked as she hugged herself in her arms for warmth. *Why did he write the words out, and why did he drop his head and kiss my hand? Ah, don't be a child!* said Jeanne-Marie now in rebuke to her. *You should know that is Bastineau's way. He is everything simple and free and gay until the real words are ready to be spoken. And he said them to you?* asked Fenton of the early morning. *Yes, he said them to me two years ago,* said Jeanne-Marie, and she added: *He didn't say them to you. But he wrote them!* Fenton cried out, and she crossed quickly to the refuge door now and opened it, and there beyond the step it was written still, frozen hard and enduring again as if forever: *Ci-gît mon coeur.*

The morning of that day, when the sun was high, was spent effacing the Austrian's steps down the long way to the glacier.

The marble highways forked at the crossroads here, and the rocks of the Trélaporte lay like islets, with the foam breaking on them, in the vast, pure flow of ice. In the afternoon, she found an Alpine guidebook in the refuge, on the kitchen shelf, and she turned the pages to the history of the Col de Géant, for Bastineau's territory lay that way.

"It is not an obvious pass when regarded from Courmayeur," the guidebook said, "and the summit cannot be seen from the Montanvert. The *cabane* lies a few feet down on the southern side, and commands a wide-flung view on Italy." *And there they are living like wild men*, she thought, and she could hear the music of their courage playing, strong, and sweet, and clear. *There are Couttet and Socquet and Ravanel, and the ones who are strangers to me—out of cities and concentration camps and across the frontiers.* On the page that followed, there was a paragraph on the icefall that lay in darkness now outside the refuge. "At the summit it is broken into transverse chasms of enormous width and depth," said the printed words, "and the ridges between these break across and form those castellated masses to which the name of *séracs* has been applied." And *Bastineau is crossing them alone*, she thought, *not roped to another man's waist, but alone out there in the silence where the fiercest cry for help would be soundless.* "In descending the cascade, the ice is crushed and riven," said the guidebook. "Ruined towers, which have tumbled from the summit, cumber the slope, and smooth vertical precipices of ice rise in succession from the ruins. At the base of the fall, the broken masses are again pressed together, but

150

the confusion is still great, and the glacier here is tossed into billowy shapes."

It was down this fall that the party of men returned on the third day. She saw the first movement of them below the ridge in the early afternoon. There were two black threads of them moving roped among the *séracs*, and as they descended slowly, with painstaking care, it could not be said if there were five or six men coming down. Now it would seem to Fenton that there were only five, and *So they have killed de Vaudois*, she thought, *and there are five men with blood on their hands descending now across the ice*. And again it would seem that there were six who came, but their progress was slow, and at times they would be lost for quarter-of-an-hour periods from sight. It was long before they took on the shape of human beings moving tentatively, warily from ridge to ridge, and now it was clear there were six of them coming, and Fenton stood on the rocks before the refuge, watching, with one hand lifted to shade her eyes.

The sun was going as they took the last flight of the cascade, and she could see them distinctly, but far still, roped three by three, with one group dragging a burden behind. Before the base, they paused, and Fenton saw the minute shapes move together, and two of the figures bend to lift and lower the burden down the precipice of ice. *There are six, de Vaudois and the five guides*, she thought. *There are six— then that is the dead they are bearing down. That is the dead boy, bound in the canvas sheet they carried up, like an arm across the shoulders. They have found him at last*, she thought, and she felt a rush of sickness in her. *De Vaudois' mission is finished—they're bringing the dead boy down.* She turned back to the refuge now, and near the step of it she halted, and she kneeled down in the snow again and touched the scarcely discernible words one man had written there. Then she laid her hands flat on the surface of them, and she pressed the letters down until nothing remained but the imprint of her own two palms upon the bluish snow.

It was another hour before Falcroz came through the refuge door, and his face was weary. His shoulders were stooped in his jacket, and he was old as he had never seemed before.

"So you found him?" said Fenton quietly from where she sat on the bench before the stove, and Falcroz pushed his hat up off his forehead, and with the back of his hand he wiped the sweat away. He shook his head slowly and wearily at her a moment before he answered:

"God help us. We found the body of Bastineau."

Five

"CHAMPAGNE!" exclaimed de Vaudois as Fenton came into the café of the hotel. "I've ordered two bottles of it!" He wore his city clothes again, his sleek bag stood at the doorway, and his overcoat was laid across his shoulders as it had been the first night in the train. "Having a little celebration before I go," he said in English to her, and he motioned to the table where Madame Perrin and Gustav sat on the leather-upholstered seat against the wall. "A farewell drink!" de Vaudois said, and he put his hand under Fenton's arm and drew her forward. The champagne bottles, packed in snow, stood in buckets on the floor.

"There won't be time. I haven't done my bags," said Fenton. She spoke in a quiet, weary voice, and her eyes on them were filled with quiet, still uncomprehending grief.

"Come!" said de Vaudois. "Your train leaves at three—mine leaves in thirty minutes." He opened the box of cigarettes before her, but she shook her head. "I'll be in Geneva for dinner tonight," he said, his spirits high. "Why don't you join me? Fresh caviar with the cocktails, and *filet mignon* at the Buffet de la Gare!"

"They're expecting me in Lyon," Fenton said.

"*B'en, mademoiselle,* at six hundred francs the bottle I'd think twice before refusing," said Gustav Perrin, and he looked up at her in blue-eyed pleasure, and he wiped his red mustaches off his mouth with the back of his hand. "We haven't seen anything like it since the defeat!"

"And we won't see anything like it after *monsieur* is gone," said Madame Perrin, and the disaster of the empty tables, the vacant hotel rooms, the tourist trade ruined now forever stood grievous in her eyes.

De Vaudois had lifted one of the bottles from its nest of snow, and he set about removing the cork with the flat of his thumb.

"Shall I do it *à la maître d'hôtel,* or let it strike the ceiling as if we were at a wedding?" he asked, and Madame Perrin clasped her plump, soiled hands together and watched the champagne bottle with delight.

"Oh, let it hit the ceiling!" she cried, but she added

154

quickly: "Unless you think it might leave a mark. We had the plaster done over in 1939, and you can't get paint any more——"

"*B'en*, if you let it fly there's a chance of losing some of it too," said her husband, and he smoothed his mustaches back in anticipation with the side of his hand.

But whatever was said, Fenton heard nothing but the voice of Falcroz speaking still in the Requin hut, giving the words of explanation, jerking them out as if from a core of actual pain: *We dug three hours, the snow was fresh and loose and went easy as snow in the spring. And then we saw the mountain boot. I knew it at once. I knew the nail formation on the sole. It couldn't be anybody's but his.* She had turned toward the stairway now, but as de Vaudois eased the cork out with his thumb, his eyes moved quickly to her.

"Come," he said. "You can't refuse! You're the guest of honor! Everything I've accomplished I owe to you!" She saw the quick, brief gleam of malice in his eye. "Six glasses," he said, and as he tipped the bottle above them, Madame Perrin and Gustav watched in wonder the miracle of their glasses brimming with clear, sparkling wine. "Six," he repeated. "Two for our hosts, one for *mademoiselle*, one for me, and two for the absent——"

"A rather mixed company," said Fenton in a low voice, and because the will for protest, for choice, for action even had lapsed from her now, she sat down at the table with the others, and blindly watched the champagne spring bubbling in the glasses' stems.

"Yes, mixed, as you say," said de Vaudois, and his voice

155

was pleasant. "But, as a neutral, I can afford to drink with the men of any nation—living or dead." He held the bottle above the last two glasses that stood empty still, and he looked at Fenton. "It seemed to me distinctly unfair to leave out of this celebration the two young men who brought us to Truex," he said, and then he paused a moment. "Your guest and mine," he said, and he filled the empty glasses to the brim. "The Swiss boy and Bastineau."

"God rest his soul," said Gustav, and he crossed himself with the fingers of one hand.

"Here's to your return, *monsieur!*" said Madame Perrin, and her eyes seemed ready to let fall their grief that the days of feasts and celebrations, of extra ration cards and black-market champagne, had now come to an end.

De Vaudois touched his glass to Madame Perrin's and to Gustav's before he took the first bright, sparkling throatful down.

"Ah, too sweet!" he said, and he made a grimace.

"*B'en*, the Maréchal says we must accept without protest what is left," said Gustav in gentle explanation. "The con-querors have taken the best," he said, and his eyes were pa-tient as he shook his head.

"I shall be back when the thaws set in, *madame*," de Vau-dois was saying. *Just to see him go,* thought Fenton in despair-ing silence. *Just to see him step into the train, and be rid of the sight and the sound of him forever.* She looked up from the untouched glass before her to the clock above the bar. Its hands marked ten minutes past eleven. There were twenty

156

minutes still before the train would go. "I can accomplish nothing further this year. I see that now," de Vaudois' voice went on with it. "The Swiss boy's body lies too deep for winter excavating———"

"But the season—the skiing season?" said Madame Perrin, and her fingers fell as if in actual hunger on his arm. "I make special rates for big parties—you know that, *monsieur*. You know I make arrangements so that everything's nice—the Maréchal's statuette in every bedroom, and nothing but Radio-Paris on the wireless. I've always conformed, haven't I, Gustav? I do everything they ask, and still I can't meet the taxes———"

"*B'en*, we'd do better working the soil like Cousin Perrin and La Cousine," said Gustav gently, and de Vaudois' face did not change as he filled their glasses again.

"Oh, there's always a way of putting something aside for yourself when you have your own produce!" said Madame Perrin, and there was a canny look in her eye as she lifted the second glass of champagne.

"That's their place above the Miraculous Calvary?" said de Vaudois. "I stopped in there for a drink of milk the other day." *In twenty minutes he will be gone*, thought Fenton. *In twenty minutes the mountains will be free of his prying and questioning at last.* "Their cattle look fat. They seem to have all they need," said de Vaudois.

"Ah, who knows what they take of the offerings for themselves!" said Madame Perrin bitterly.

"*B'en*, what do you know of them, woman?" Gustav cried

out in sudden heat. "You've not said the *bon jour* to them up there on the mountain since the quarrel about the goat in 1932!"

"And whose fault was it about the price of the goat!" cried Madame Perrin.

"There's no harm done," said de Vaudois, and he lifted the second bottle from its bed of snow. "So your vacation is over," he said to Fenton, "and we take our separate directions. You one way, and I the other. But you, at least, have the end of your story." He held the bottle against him and pressed at the cork with his thumb. "One more name will be carved on the monument to the dead, and now Mass can be said for him. I hear Bastineau's people are coming up from the valley tomorrow. You're not staying over for the funeral?" he said.

"Tomorrow I shall be back in Lyon," said Fenton, and her voice was quiet. *In thirteen minutes,* she said in silence, *he will go and the village's grief will be its own grief, untampered with at last.*

De Vaudois shot the cork out recklessly, and it struck the ceiling overhead, and the delicate, gold foam spilled swiftly from the bottle's mouth into the glasses below.

"Let us drink this time to the dead!" de Vaudois said then, and he lifted his glass. "To the Swiss boy and Bastineau!" Madame Perrin and Gustav raised their glasses and gravely drank, but Fenton sat motionless, her eyes in blank, speechless grief on the empty street beyond the café's glass. "Those two young men," said de Vaudois, standing still, "are symbols to me of this entire conflict's absurdity. Were they alive, they would have been seated here as friends with us—discussed

158

skiing, rock-climbing, mountaineering feats, the weather, clouds, stars. But, instead——" He shrugged his shoulders. "Let us speak the truth among ourselves, at least," he said. "France misled, deceived, was made a party to the declaration of England's war——"

"Ah, I always said that," said Madame Perrin, wisely, "although the English tourist trade was something to count on——"

"Those two dead young men," said de Vaudois, the glass stem in which the fluid sparkled held in his hand, "might have been sitting here with us, at this table, if the population of this village—and all the villages of France—had recognized and accepted without protest the inevitability of what is to be established on European soil. There is to be order—order, Madame Perrin, such as you and others of discrimination feel the lack of here. I shall come back, for my work here is not finished. I shall come back to find that Swiss boy, and to avenge his life——"

He drained his glass quickly then, and he made a grimace at the taste. Madame Perrin and Gustav stood up in respect as he thrust his arms into the sleeves of his coat and settled the velvet collar at his neck.

"*Monsieur*, you have promised to return for the season!" Madame Perrin said in distress. "You have the folders? Special terms for long stays and big parties——"

"I give you my word," said de Vaudois, and he shook her hand. "Every room in the hotel shall be filled for you this winter. You may count on it," he said.

"*B'en*, we'll be glad to welcome you back," said Gustav

gently, and de Vaudois turned to Fenton. She was standing, buttoning her coat across.

"I'll walk to the station with you." *For the sake of the men on the frontier still, I'll walk to the station with you. I'll touch your hand as if you were friend, and I'll stand on the platform watching. For the sake of the men they haven't killed yet, I'll see with my own eyes that you go.* "You have five minutes still," she said.

For a little while after the train had moved off from the station platform and taken the curve in the high, rocky land, Fenton stood motionless on the weathered boards. She stood looking at the tracks down which the train had moved. *He is gone, he has left the mountains,* and now the peace and quiet of the heights spread suddenly pure and strong around her. *He is gone. Now even the dead may lie quiet in their graves.* As she crossed the square before the statue of the mountaineer, the air seemed clearer, fresher on her face, and the statue on its rock stood poised as if for action, the bronze hand lifted to shade its steady eyes. *I am a part of what they have died for,* she said as she blindly took the direction of the village street. *I am a part of the fearless dream that Bastineau and his country dreamed together. He has taught me the words to speak and the acts to give to a nation's protest. Let me be strong enough to make use of them! Whatever has happened, let me be strong enough to carry them back to Lyon with me, not to leave here empty-handed as I came.*

She walked down the cobbled lane between the ancient

walls where the lizards ran quick in summer, and only when she saw the arch of the church's door ahead did she know that it was to sit for a moment in the church's quiet that she had come this way. She mounted the shallow, footworn steps, and touched the iron handle, and the door moved slowly inward to the odor of sanctity and damp and fragrant stone. The light of the November noon came bleak as dawn through the tall, stained windows, and Fenton felt a tremor of cold run through her blood as she moved down the aisle, with her footsteps echoing through the silent nave. There were no candles lit at the altars or in the chapels, and the rush-bottomed praying chairs and the pews stood empty. The columns planted at the pews' ends were strong, and thick, and Gothic, and Fenton passed between them and sat down in the shadow of the carved pulpit stage. *The quiet here will give me strength,* she said in silence, and she bowed her face in her hands, so that she did not see the man who had crossed quickly before the altar, nor did she hear his step until it sounded, suddenly close, upon the flaggings' stone. Then she lifted her head and looked up, startled, at him. It was *monsieur le curé*, fleshless, perishable, it seemed, as the likeness of a saint stepped from a stained-glass window in the church's wall.

"This morning you made your farewells to Père Chatelard and the others," he said. "I was waiting for you to come to me." His voice was low, his face the texture of parchment in the church's twilight. "Dizot and Perrin have watched over the body in the crypt all night," he said. He stood there, one narrow, frail hand extended to her—not man, it seemed, but the essence of man's spirit carved in another century upon the portal of a church and given life now by its own intensity. "Come, we shall pray for the dead together," he said.

Fenton rose, suddenly trembling, to follow him, and as they passed the altar he paused and crossed himself and touched his knee in reverence to the stone. They walked past the choir in silence, and at the descent of the spiral stairs, he halted and turned to her again.

"*Mon père*, help me—show me how to be brave!" she cried out in a soft, broken voice to him, and now she felt the tears rush from her eyes.

"Listen, my child," he said, and he laid his hand on her shoulder. "Everything has its reason, its absolute purpose, however bitterly the meaning may be concealed. There is no cause for grief. Do you understand me?"

"I have tried—I have tried to say these things———" whispered Fenton, and the taste of tears was bitter in her mouth.

"Bastineau has died many deaths," said the curé, and his face seemed luminous now in the semidark. "The first one in the schrund, at the hands of the Fascisti, in the week of Pétain's armistice. He has been dead to his people—dead to any home to which he might return—dead to a church to kneel down in. He has been dead to the love of a woman—and this is anguish to a young man. But he died so that some portion of his nation's honor might survive." The dark, brilliant eyes before her burned into hers, no longer the flesh's but the spirit's vehicles of sight. The voice that spoke came strongly from the erect, slight frame, and the bones themselves seemed vibrant with its power, like music passing richly through a violin's fragile shell. "Bastineau has died before," he said. "This time he died in the avalanche. He died again so that strangers would leave the mountains in peace——"

"But died——" repeated Fenton in wonder. "Died, *mon père*? You say it—you say it as if it were somehow not a final death?" she said.

"Come," said the curé again, and he turned and, lifting the black skirt of his cassock in one hand, he started the descent of the stairs. Below there were candles burning in the crypt, so that the way was not obscure. At the last turn of the spiral, Fenton saw from the step behind him that the uncovered coffin stood on a couch of stone, and the flames of the candles set at the head and feet quivered upright in the sepulcher's dark. "Falcroz designed this death," said the curé in a low voice, and he paused now at the foot of the stairs. "The guides were to excavate," he said, "and if in the end the snow revealed nothing, then they would come down empty-handed as they had before." He crossed the flaggings to the crypt's radiant heart where the candles burned as if upon a brilliant stage, and the shadows stood at the outskirts like an audience waiting in the darkened stalls. Fenton came slowly, breathlessly behind him, the tears dry on her face, and at the brink of the incandescence, the curé paused again and turned to take her hand. "Come," he said gently, and they stood before the open coffin together, and he drew the sheet back from the figure that lay within.

As he drew it back from the face, Fenton held to the curé's arm for strength, and then the breath stood halted in her mouth as she saw the strands of fine, blond hair which fell

163

across the dead man's brow. The cloth moved slowly in the curé's hand, and she looked tremblingly down upon the lashes standing stiff and light-colored as corn along the closed, bluish lids, upon the pinched, dark nostrils, the bruised, inflexible mouth, and on the light stubble that covered the round, clefted chin. No effort had been made, it seemed, to prepare him for eternity—except that a crucifix had been set between the fingers which lay clasped upon the stony breast. He wore the climbing jacket still, with the loden stuff of it ripped across one shoulder—lying there, a blond young stranger frozen and preserved in death, with no vestige of youth's recklessness remaining to him now.

"But—it isn't Bastineau," whispered Fenton in awe. "It has nothing to do with Bastineau."

"It is not Bastineau. It was never Bastineau," said the curé, and he drew the cloth again across the features of the dead. "Falcroz designed it so," he said in the same low voice as he turned from the coffin. "They led de Vaudois to the avalanche, not believing it was for the body of a Swiss boy, but for the living that de Vaudois had come." The curé had begun to walk slowly, with silent, measured step, back and forth in the crypt now, his frail hands clasped behind him where the shabby fringes of his sash hung down. "They went up to the avalanche with him, saying nothing, but believing that he had come here to track down the leader of frontier resistance, exactly as the Swiss boy, posing as an excursionist, had come. They believed he was after Bastineau," said the curé. "Very well, then, Falcroz instructed the other guides, if a body were found in the avalanche, let it be that of Bastineau."

"But one look at the face of the dead man would have told him!" said Fenton.

"Remember," said *monsieur le curé*, "that de Vaudois had never seen either the Swiss boy or Bastineau. Falcroz believed that de Vaudois would not leave Truex until he had found the man he wanted. And the man he wanted was not a dead boy. The man he wanted was Bastineau." The curé stopped pacing the flaggings of the crypt for a moment, and one hand fingered the beads which hung in the dark folds of his dress. "So there is the proof for him," he said, and he gestured toward the refulgence in which the coffin lay.

"But de Vaudois has solved nothing. He is not a fool. He will come back!" Fenton cried softly.

"In the meantime, he has left," said the curé. "For the moment, that is enough. We have let him come and go in peace. He has found out nothing. Had we harmed him, rid ourselves of him as we did of the Swiss before him, the alarm would have been given. Two agents gone—one after another. They would have walked in on us, seized hostages, and this source of supply would have been wiped out for the men on the frontier."

"But Bastineau——" said Fenton in sudden helplessness. "Who is to be told the truth? Is the whole village to mourn for him now as dead? His people are coming up from the valley for the funeral—there is talk of inscribing his name on the monument with those of the others——"

"My child," said the curé, and now he was pacing the stone again, "Dizot and Perrin watched the night here, and they are sworn to silence. They and the guides will never speak.

165

For the village, for the entire valley, for his family, for the Church even, this dead man in the coffin will be buried in hallowed ground tomorrow as Gabriel Bastineau."

"But his sisters!" Fenton cried out in protest.

"Women talk," said the curé. "They cannot know."

"I am a woman. Why have you told the truth to me?" asked Fenton.

"You set mother and father aside to return to us," said the curé, and as he stopped before her again his voice was fervent. "You came back because this was your soil and these your people. You returned to us, bringing nourishment, succor. Even with years and a vast sea between us, our cause was your cause. You came back to fight with us. You set the rest aside."

"I came back to find Bastineau," said Fenton, and she lifted her head and met his eyes.

"Yes," said the curé, "that was perhaps the name you gave it. But you came back because your heart would not lie still within you, as the hearts of all of us who care will not lie still. Because of this I have told you that Bastineau is not dead— because of this, and because you are leaving Truex. Your joy will not be present among us to be recorded. You are going back to Lyon—but Bastineau's family remain near us, and they will be watched, they are watched already. Come, we will extinguish the candles together," he said, and he turned again to the coffin. "It is not their light at this late hour which can illuminate a heretic's way." He pinched the first wick out between forefinger and thumb, and Fenton moved to the other side and blew quickly at the separate tongues of flame. "I shall watch here throughout the day," said the curé, proceeding from candle to candle in the darkening crypt, "for no man or woman must see his face. Dizot and La Cousine will watch through the night. Tomorrow night, after the funeral, the guides will open the grave again and remove the body while the village sleeps."

"Remove it?" said Fenton quickly.

"It may not rest in consecrated ground," the curé said. "Only the bones of the good lie there, not the evil. You will remember the Bishop of Brussels' decree this year—that a Belgian who accepts to wear the German uniform and fights as a German on any front may no longer be accorded the last sacrament, nor may his body lie in hallowed ground." He snuffed the final candle out, and they were left in darkness. "These men have put their faith in a leader who swears he will wipe the ten commandments from the earth," the curé said.

It was only as she followed him up the spiral stairs into the twilight of the church's nave that the realization of the truth came suddenly alive within her. *Bastineau is not dead!* the solemn stillness cried aloud. *Bastineau is in the mountains still, crossing the glaciers, leaping the crevasses, the nails of his boots holding firm on ice or snow! Bastineau didn't die this year or last!* played the silent organ, and as Fenton and the curé passed the choir, it seemed to her that a thousand voices broke into clear, sweet song. *Bastineau is alive, nothing is ended!* rang the ancient flaggings as they crossed them. *He will be at the Montanvert tonight—the eighth of November. Tonight I shall see his face again, and hear his voice, and touch his hand!*

167

"Now you may go in peace to Lyon," said the curé at the doorway, and Fenton turned quickly and looked into his eyes.

"Tomorrow," she said. "Things have altered. Tonight I shall climb the mountain to receive my orders."

"Do not let the joy be written too clearly in your face," said the curé gently, and they held each other's hands an instant. "Extinguish it for a little, as we did the candles' flames."

It was dark when she put her climbing things on and started up the mountain path, but she knew, stone by stone, and turn by turn, the way she had to go. The night was clear, and the stars were close, and in all the stillness there was no sound but the crunch and slip of her boots as she climbed upward in the snow. Here in the forest, it had melted little, and she mounted slowly, her breath coming even and warm, but her heart was quick with elation in her. *I've raced Bastineau down here, coming back from the glaciers on summer nights,* she thought, with the air cold on her face now. *And once when we went up at dawn, Father was with us, and Castor and Pollux were high in the heavens, and Bastineau dropped back behind the others to walk with me and say their names aloud.* More than two hours had elapsed before the surface of the sky expanded, and the stars became more myriad ahead as the timber thinned, and then, as the tree line dropped behind, she felt the presence of the glacier, unseen, but marvelously and icily there. Another twenty minutes passed before she rounded the turn in the path, and there in the dark stood the Montanvert, square and prisonlike in the silence, and against the high, luminous

168

constellations rose in bleak warning the stone needles of the Dru.

Fenton crossed the wide platform of land toward the block of the Montanvert's façade, and once she had reached the building's terrace, her footsteps rang aloud on the stone. She knew where the door would be, and she felt for the window to the right of it, and her fingers groped for the key along its ledge. When she found it, she fitted it into the great door's lock, and as the door opened inward, the cold of the abandoned house was sudden as lake water on her flesh, and it shook her to the bone. I shall wait outside until he comes, she thought, and she crossed the platform of land again to the wall that had been built above the precipitous drop to the glacier's bed. She leaned her arms in her jacket on the stone, and there lay the broad, white highway of abysmal ice just visible in the starlight below. *People have come here filled with hope and youth*, thought Fenton. *They have stood on the brink of the glacier and felt its power as I feel it now. The Empress Eugénie came here and paused and looked down on its ice, and Napoléon III, and a thousand nameless climbers, stopping for breath here before going the rest of the way.* There it lay, the static likeness of a river halted in its turbulent descent, carved monstrously still below. *It is ice*, she thought, *and it gives back no reflection of our faces. If we call down to it, it is not the sound of our own voices that answers, but the cold, clear echo of the cries of the others who have perished there. We are of the same company, the dead and the living, drawn to ice, held by it,* and she shivered again with cold as she leaned on the stone.

And then, without warning, she heard the voice singing. It seemed to rise from the glacier itself, but in a moment she knew that it came from the path that wound up from below. *"L'Infant'rie Alpine, voilà mes amours!"* were the words sung aloud in the night. *"Et je l'aimerai, je l'aimerai sans cess-e!"*; and the voice was Bastineau's. He was mounting quickly, unseen in the dark, and as she turned from the wall toward the direction in which he would come, she felt the wondrous sense of joy rise in her. *And it can never be any different*, she thought, *not for Jeanne-Marie's sake or anyone else's. It can never be any different no matter what happens in any country or however old I grow.* It was ten minutes before he gained the flat of the land, and she called his name out across the darkness.

"Bastineau! *Salut!*" she said, and now he stood beside her, head and shoulders taller than she, close and warm and living in the glacial night.

"*Salut!*" said Bastineau, and his breath came evenly although he had been climbing fast. "I arranged the stars and the singing for you."

"Thank you," said Fenton, and they did not touch each other's hands.

They walked toward the dark shape of the building side by side, not speaking. He went first through the open door, and he ran against a chair in the darkness, and then he pushed it out of her way, its legs crying out as it scraped across the stone.

"I'm going to risk a fire," he said, and he closed and locked the door against the outer cold. "At the other end, there's a fireplace," he said, and he moved quickly past her. "I knew where the wood was six months ago." She followed the voice and the footsteps that rang loud and strong and fearless down the corridor, and, as they passed them one by one, she knew where the archways of the doors must stand. Here was the high-ceilinged dining room where tourists had stood waiting for the white-clothed tables in other years, and here the guides' messroom where the ruder tables and the long wooden benches were and where the ice axes had hung. Here, on the other side, was the door to the hotel kitchen, and, farther, the arch into the café where you drank your glass of red wine when you came down from the heights, weary and your skin burned black and the core of contentment basking in you.

When he reached the end of the hall, Bastineau took the matches from his pocket, and he struck one on the open chimney's stone. For an instant, standing close in the dark, the little handful of light was flung into their faces. "De Vaudois?" he asked at once, but his eyes had nothing to do with the question's vigilance. They were moving in something like tenderness on the sight of her standing there.

"Gone since this morning," she said. "I saw him off. He took the train at half-past eleven." She paused a moment. "He drank your health in champagne before he left," she said.

"Good," said Bastineau, and she saw the white of his teeth for a moment as he smiled, and then the match expired in his hand.

"Bastineau," she said quickly to the darkness. "Don't die any more. I can't bear it."

"I haven't any intention of dying," he said, and he struck another match on the stone.

171

"But they found you two days ago, killed by the avalanche," said Fenton, and Bastineau, squatting before the chimney now, looked up at her, and he was laughing.

"*Tiens!*" he said. He shifted the heavy logs into place. "I didn't know it. I've seen no one from below."

"Falcroz arranged it," she said, standing on the hearth. "The Swiss boy's body became yours. De Vaudois seemed pleased—elated, even. He left immediately."

"There'll be others like him after us," said Bastineau. He put the match to the paper and the fans of brush beneath the wood. "You gave me his sister's address at the Requin. We have the information on it. It's Gestapo headquarters in Geneva," he said.

"And I was a part of it! I was to let them know if he didn't come down alive!" said Fenton. Bastineau squatted before the fire on his thighs, and Fenton sat down on the stone step at the corner of the chimney now and watched the side of his face outlined against the blaze. "Bastineau, I'm leaving for Lyon tomorrow," she said. "I thought you could tell me what there is that I could do."

He did not turn his head when she spoke, but he squatted there still, his hands dropped loose between his knees, watching the flame.

"I hadn't thought of you going back," he said. "I don't know why I hadn't thought of it at all."

"They're few enough of us to do the work. They need me," she said. She looked at the line of the nose and chin, and the thick, black hair that sprang back from the brow in the fire's light. "I'll have to leave tomorrow," she said.

172

"Tomorrow?" he said quickly, and still he did not look at her, but she felt her heart falter an instant at the sudden sound of pain.

"But perhaps there—perhaps in Lyon, there would be some way for me to help—to serve as well," she said. "If you could tell me what to do—how I could do it——"

"Tomorrow," he said again. "I hadn't thought of that. I'd thought of you staying here," he said, and he did not move, but squatted there, his eyes steady on the fire.

"But here?" asked Fenton in bewilderment.

"I know. *C'est fou*," he said, and he gestured it aside. Then he stretched his legs out, and he lay full length before the fire, leaning back upon his elbow before the blazing hearth. It might have been some other year, she thought, and they just down from skiing, sitting talking like this before the chalet's hearth; it might have been peacetime, and the climb from Italy done that afternoon, and now they were resting from the long way they had come. "Yes, Lyon," he said, looking musingly at the fire. "There is sometimes trouble—sometimes a break there in the chain."

"Tell me what I can do," said Fenton, and she watched his face.

"It is like this," he said, and as he talked his eyes were on the fire, and the light of it polished his brow, and his straight, bronzed nose, and touched his lips with flame. "We get the men across the frontier, but that's just the beginning for them. They have to get farther—in market carts, by bicycle, on foot, jumping trains when they can do it, getting through France with faked papers or with none at all, and their pockets nearly empty. Sometimes they speak the language and sometimes they don't, and Lyon—like every other part of the country—is a wilderness to them." He had picked up a bit of bark from the floor, and he slowly splintered it in his fingers as he talked. "Jeanne-Marie sees to the money for them to carry with them and see them through, and the papers when she can manage it," he said, and his voice had not altered, his eyes had not wavered from the fire as he spoke the other woman's name. "Money and papers, either are hard to come by," he said, "and if they get through to Lyon they have to find the men of the *service* there. There's Bosquet, in the Cours Lafayette," he said, and he told the number to her.

She took the end of pencil and the notebook from her jacket pocket.

"Bosquet, Cours Lafayette," she said, and she wrote it down.

"There's Frassinet on the Place de la Bourse," he said, and he told the names of the others to her. "When the secret police or the gendarmes get suspicious, they have to shift bases, and there's where the men we send go wrong. Those addresses were good last week, but from day to day we can't be certain. If there's trouble, and we don't know it in time, it's these men who've crossed the frontier who pay for it," he said. "They follow our directions, but if Bosquet or Frassinet or any others of the *service* have had to jump, they're finished. It's the police instead who are waiting for them there." He tossed the little handful of crumbled bark onto the fire, and then he went on saying to her: "You could be a strong link. Established there already, covered by the legitimate work you're doing——"

"Yes," said Fenton. "Tell me what I am to do."

"From Lyon," said Bastineau, and he was on his knees now, reaching for another log, and he cast it in upon the others. "From Lyon, they make Marseille," he said. He watched the half-burned wood in the chimney explode softly into sparks and fresh, delicate bursts of flame, and then he brushed his hands off and stretched out again upon the floor. "Canal boats down the Rhone, truck traffic, freight car," he said. "It varies. One night it's this, and one night another, but with luck they make it. When you get back to Lyon, talk to Frassinet, Bosquet, any of the others. They'll give you the *combines*. In Marseille, there's a place on the Vieux Port—you'll get the exact indications from the *service*. They sign them up on cargo boats for Casablanca, get them French papers, ship them out. From this end," he said, "we'll give you as first contact in Lyon. Write the address down and the hours you're working there." At the last, he said: "That's the story. We've been getting them through for three years now—anti-Fascists out of Italy, Austrians, Poles, Czechs, Hungarians, even German refugees who want to wear a uniform and fight." *Drop by drop*, he might have been saying, *drop by drop the blood of the conquered countries is dripping from their severed veins; drop by drop it is accumulating, as waters press at a dam head; drop by drop, it is rising in a deep, vindictive tide.* "There's a group of men, Frenchmen, coming across the frontier tonight," he said. "Prisoners escaped from Germany and getting back."

"And you?" said Fenton across the firelight to him.

"I'm going up. I have to bring them down," he said. "Swiss maneuvers on the Glacier de Saleinaz have thrown them off the usual route, so they'll cross by the Col des Hirondelles. I'll have to be moving up," he said.

"I didn't mean that," said Fenton. "I was trying to say, you—you, Bastineau, will you ever be able to escape, yourself? Will you be able to get out in the end?"

He stood up now, and he stretched his arms in the fire's heat a moment, and then he leaned, at ease, against the mantel's stone.

"I know the snow, I know the glaciers. I'm needed here," he said.

She sat quiet an instant on the step of the hearth below him, her hands clasped tightly around her knees.

"Bastineau, I'm afraid for you," she said abruptly then, and she looked up into his face. He was buttoning his jacket over, turning the collar of it up, and his eyes and teeth in the fire's light shone hard and bright as snow.

"I brought you up," he said, and his voice was quiet. "You're not afraid of anything," he said.

She got to her feet, and her hands were in her trousers' pockets, and with the toe of one boot she scattered the smoldering logs apart.

"I'll wait until the fire has burned lower," she said, and when she turned to look at him, he took the two swift steps to her, and he took her face between his hands, with the hair pushed back on his fingers, and he held it steadily there.

"Fenton," he said, and his voice had altered. "Will you say it just once to me again? Will you say it before I go?"

Her eyes were fixed, almost in fright, on his eyes, and the breath had gone from her heart, and she could not speak aloud.

"Bastineau, what is it you want me to say?" she whispered.

"You were fifteen that spring," he was saying, and his voice was savage and tender, and his mouth was soft and reckless with love. "I've never forgotten the sound of it, never. That night of the thaw, when the white horse threw you, and I picked you up and carried you home, you said it then. You said, 'Bastineau, I love you.'"

She did not know for how long she felt the bliss and the wonder of it, and then suddenly she saw the fire clearly again, and the stone of the chimneyplace, and the edge of darkness stopped short by the fire's light. There was strength in her hands again, and she laid them hard against him, and she stepped back from him, trembling, and shook her head fiercely free.

"You can't be like this! You can't say these things!" she cried out, and she heard the grief in her own voice as she said it. "You can't be everything to everyone! You have to have some kind of loyalty!" she said. She could see the hunting horn of the Alpine Infantry in silver at Jeanne-Marie's throat, and Jeanne-Marie's voice was saying the words to her again. "I've believed too much in you—hero-worship, crazy schoolgirl business!" Fenton cried out, and she could not stop the rushing anguish of it now. "You've been everything for too many years—I don't want to stop believing in you——" And *Why can't he leave me? Why can't he walk down the hall and out the door?* her heart cried wildly in her. *Will he stand there looking at me like this until I can't keep the crying back?* "You've been everything—Christmas Eve and Easter morning and the Fourteenth of July—crazy, I know," she said, and her hands were clenched hard at her sides, and her teeth were shaking as if from the cold. "You were something I should have outgrown in my teens, but I didn't. You called me your child. Maybe I was once, Bastineau, but I'm not any longer. I've grown up. You don't believe it. I'm a woman now —don't you see I'm a woman? I'm a woman, and you belong to another woman," she said.

Afterward she could not say what the look was in his face —whether bewilderment, or outrage, or incredible pain. He had opened his hands blindly, almost in helplessness, as she spoke, and now, without warning, he threw back his head in the firelight, and he began to laugh aloud.

"I?" he said. "I? I belong to a woman?" He brought the tough, broad palms of his hands up to his breast, and he pressed them there as if for breath, for his laughing was not done. "I belong to a woman?" he said again, his voice incredulous. His teeth were white, and his throat seemed ready to split with laughter, and then suddenly she saw the look of anger that lit in his eye. "No, I have been saved from that— that much I have been spared!" he said, and the laughter had ceased. "I was about to make an offer—here, tonight, in this room—but because I've never asked any woman before, it didn't come easily to the tongue! 'I have an established position, a steady income, an assured future,' I was about to say, but you saved me from it. 'I'm quite a catch,' I might have said, but I didn't have the audacity for it——"

"But Jeanne-Marie!" Fenton said bitterly to him. She stood with her back to the dying fire, her eyes in quiet impeachment on him. "You and Jeanne-Marie are to be married," she said.

"Stop," said Bastineau, and he took a step toward her, his voice furious and low. "I don't know what lies they've told you—I haven't the time or the patience to hear what they've said! But if you want to leave me anything to go up the glaciers with tonight, stop what you're saying." He stood head and shoulders above her, his eyes in fury on her, his breath hot on her hair. "After all the years, winter and summer, day and night!" he said, speaking quickly, savagely to her. "Since you were fifteen, it's been music playing, it's been my girl saying that thing to me in the cold and the dark and the solitude up there! When they'd shoot a man crossing the frontier, I'd cry like a kid in my bunk at night, and my girl would be there, and she'd say it again to me the way she said it when I carried her up the road, and nothing else mattered except those words she was saying in comfort to my heart. Sometimes the food didn't come through, ten days at a stretch," he said, saying it furiously at her, "and we'd sit in the hut with the blizzard outside wiping out hope and courage and all the other fine things that men are supposed to have! And she'd say it again, and because she'd say it—not words like anybody's words, but my girl speaking to me, I could pull the belt a hole tighter and wait, I could blow on my fingers and sing like a fool in spite of the cold! Nothing belongs to me!" he said fiercely. "I've got nothing to offer anyone. I own nothing—not even the clothes I wear! There's no roof over my head, I've forgotten the look of money. But this other thing—it's mine!" he said, and he struck his fist against his breast. "It crosses the glaciers with me and jumps the crevasses, it lies down to sleep at night in my arms!"

179

And then he was gone; he turned swiftly into the corridor's dark, and Fenton stood stunned an instant, her blood halted in her body, her tongue gone dry and speechless in her mouth. The sound of his footsteps died quickly in the hall, and then the clap of the outer door released her as if a hand had struck her face, and she called out his name.

"Bastineau, Bastineau, oh, damn you, Bastineau, my love!" she cried, and she was running now, calling his name aloud. She was out of the dying fire's light, she had almost reached the corridor's tunnel of complete obscurity, and there she stopped short, for a man was standing, lighting a cigarette, not two yards from her in the tunnel's dark. She saw the stiff felt hat, with the bit of pheasant feather stuck in the ribbon of it, and for a moment she did not see the features of his face, for his head was lowered to the lighter's flame. Then he snapped the lighter closed and dropped it into his jacket pocket.

"I wouldn't go any farther if I were you," said de Vaudois in English to her. "I have a pistol in my other hand."

Fenton stood facing him, the pulse striking hard and quick in her throat, and then she thrust her hands down into her pockets and held them, trembling, there.

"Where have you come from?" she said, and the sound of it, in her own ears even, was the sound of a weak woman's voice speaking out of fear. *I brought you up*, said Bastineau, *nourished you, poured my courage into your veins, gave you the spirit and pride to meet them eye to eye.* "How long have you been here?" she said, and now she was not afraid any longer.

"We came up at approximately the same time," said de Vaudois, and he was approaching the edge of the fire's light, gesturing her before him as he came. "I should say I was just a little behind you in the climb."

"You mean, you followed me up?" she said.

"As well as I could," said de Vaudois, speaking English still. "You climb faster than I do. Besides, I'm in city clothes." The pistol was in his right hand now, small, short-muzzled, compact, and he motioned with it toward the hearth. "Sit down again, if you like," he said. "I'm in no particular hurry. We may as well straighten out a few points before we go down." But Fenton did not move from where she stood by the chimney, her hands in her pockets, her eyes on every movement that he made. *If he puts that down for an instant*, she thought, *I can make the hallway. He doesn't move fast, and he'll fumble in the darkness. If I can get into the hall, the door will be easy. But then, which way for help to stop him? Up the glacier after Bastineau*, she thought in desperation, *or down the mountain to the guides' café?* In the little glow from the fire that was left, she watched de Vaudois stoop and lift the last remaining log—raise it with effort from the stone, and fling it in upon the others. But in the moment that she spun toward the dark, he leapt for it before her, and he was there, breathing hard, but there with the pistol black and evil in his hand. "And then what?" he said. "Suppose you did get away. What would you do then? I've got everything I want written down here in black and white," he said, and one hand touched his breast pocket. "Bosquet in the Cours Lafayette, Frassinet on the Place de la Bourse,

181

and all the others. I've got exactly what I came to Truex for," he said.

"When did you change your mind about leaving?" Fenton asked. She was back by the fireplace again, her hands in her pockets, her boot tapping nervously against the stone.

"I didn't. Not for a moment," said de Vaudois. He watched her sit down at the corner of the hearth again.

"You mean, when you took the train this morning you knew you were going to do this tonight?" Fenton said.

"To a certain extent," said de Vaudois. He opened the box of cigarettes before her, but she shook her head. "I thought you would act with greater freedom if you believed I had left Truex." He took a fresh cigarette from the box, and he lit it, and the watch gleamed on his wrist with the light of the reviving fire as he dropped his lighter into his pocket again. "The first night we sat in the guides' café together," he said, "I came to a conclusion. I decided that if I didn't lose sight of you for an instant, it would be you who would lead me in the end to Bastineau."

"So you came back to watch me?" said Fenton bitterly, and *What a fool, what a fool I have been!* she thought as she watched the flame spread on the wood. *It is I who have led him here!*

"I got off the train at Les Houches this morning," de Vaudois said. "It was quite a pleasant walk back. I stopped in at a roadhouse for lunch on the way." He looked at the ash on the end of his cigarette an instant before he went on saying: "Madame Perrin was kind enough to tell me that you, after all, had not taken the train at three. So I kept out of sight until you started up tonight. I was just behind you. When you went over to inspect the glacier, I felt a bit chilly, so I stepped inside."

"So you were here from the beginning?" said Fenton.

"From the beginning," de Vaudois said. He knocked the ash from his cigarette with the tip of his finger. "Excuse my intrusion on the love scene," he said, and Fenton kept her eyes on the fire so as not to see the implications of his smile. "*À propos*," he said, "I'm surprised that neither of you saw through Jeanne-Marie's story. That—like the fable of Bastineau's death—was merely one more attempt to discourage your staying here. Bastineau—your Bastineau!—engaged to marry another woman! Obviously, why should you stay?"

Can this be the explanation of it—can this be it? thought Fenton, and her blood ran quick in her veins an instant, but her voice was cold, dispassionate, when she spoke aloud.

"And what will you do now?"

"I shall bury the dead," de Vaudois said quietly.

"He was Boche—that boy. Is that true, too?" asked Fenton.

De Vaudois flung his half-smoked cigarette away.

"Boche!" he repeated. "Boche!" and the color had gone in anger from his face. "In the Occupied Zone, there's a five-hundred-franc fine for the use of that word!" he said.

"Boche—both you and he Boche!" said Fenton, looking musingly at the fire still. "That's a thousand francs I owe you," she said.

"It might be simpler," said de Vaudois, and his voice was tense, "if we settled that debt in some other way."

183

"You mean, shoot me?" said Fenton, watching the fire. "But then if you did some of the glory of your triumph would be gone. It's not every day that you can turn over to the Gestapo someone with American blood still running in his veins."

"To the Gestapo!" said de Vaudois. "More correctly, to headquarters. I could scarcely turn you over to myself," he said. He selected another cigarette, and he put the flame of his lighter to it. "The American will-to-believe the good and the best has always touched me," he said. "The Swiss watch-maker story was plausible enough, I suppose, but what about cigarettes such as these?" He held it up between his fingers. "And the extra ration cards—every German has three of them to a Frenchman's one, as a matter of justice. What about the climbing shoes you have on your feet? Could a Swiss have got them? And champagne at six hundred-odd francs a bottle! Did it never occur to you that there's only one nation in Europe who can play the philanthropist this year?"

"And even Madame Perrin asked you no questions?" asked Fenton in bitterness again.

"Questions don't pay. Clients do. Madame Perrin is a hotelkeeper," de Vaudois said. He had buttoned his overcoat over now, and he dropped his right hand in the pocket of it. "Shall we make our last descent together?" he said.

"But I'm not going," said Fenton. "I intend to stay here."

"As a matter of fact, it wouldn't alter things very much if we both stayed here," said de Vaudois. He had turned and picked up a mountaineering rope from the table behind him in the dark, and now he stood uncoiling it with awkward, in-

184

experienced hands. "I've left a letter with Madame Perrin, addressed to my sister," he said. "She is to mail it tomorrow morning if I don't come down. It contains all the information necessary for the complete purge of Truex—a list of the partisans, their associates, their activities. It mentions *monsieur le curé* and his sermons, which are—as we all know— the BBC and Radio-Boston broadcasts given to the congregation in code. It includes Père Chatelard, Jacqueminot, Jeanne-Marie Favret, Cousin Perrin, Dizot, and, of course, La Cousine." He stood unwinding the lengths of rope. "It describes the Miracles of the Calvary, and indicates the principal meeting places—the guides' café, the Requin hut——"

"The Requin hut?" repeated Fenton.

"Yes, the Requin hut," said de Vaudois, and he was seeking to make a mountaineer's slipknot in the rope now. "We left you there while we climbed higher, if you remember. Falcroz led us up to the avalanche, and we were gone two days and a half." He seemed to have accomplished now what he wished with the rope, and he laid it aside for a moment. "In that time, someone joined you at the Requin," he said to Fenton, and he put his hand in his overcoat pocket and took a Norwegian mitten out. "Bastineau, or whoever it was," he said, "he dropped it on the way."

The Austrian with the Oxford accent! His second mitten! thought Fenton, but nothing altered in her eyes.

"What made you think then," she said, "that it might have been Bastineau?"

"Because I never believed in his death," he said, "and because of the eagerness with which Falcroz deliberately killed

185

him off a second time before me. That body in the avalanche——" He shook his head. "Sometimes I wonder what
kind of fools they take us for," he said.

"But if he's the man you're after, then why didn't you kill
him here tonight? You had the chance," said Fenton.

"Because I prefer to come back with sufficient numbers to
get him and the others—and to get Bastineau alive," de
Vaudois said. "This is merely a little scouting expedition that
I'm on—a quite peaceful one," he said. He had picked up
the rope again, and now he walked toward her. "The serious
business begins later. Under pressure, Bastineau should be
able to give us every detail that we need. I don't want to be
unpleasant," he said as he halted before her, "but I think
we had better go down roped. I'm armed, remember, and
I shall be behind you. You'll lead the way."

Fenton stood up by the chimney, her hands in her pockets,
watching his face. *He has the names of them all—the addresses in Lyon, the ways of escape. There must be a way to
stop him. There must be a way.* She stood there motionless,
watching his hands unwind the rope before her.

"I've got friends in the village," she said, and she heard
the note of panic in it.

"Your friends are French," said de Vaudois, and he slipped
the rope over her head, spreading it wide to pass the shoulders. "The French are scarcely in authority." He had made
the double loop around her, drawing it cruelly at the waist,
with no knot for her to fumble in the dark, and then he
brought the rope's two ends beneath his overcoat and tied
them firmly there. "We'll go straight to the *gendarmerie*,"

186

he said, and he coiled up the rope's waste length between them in his hands.

"They're Frenchmen, too, the gendarmes," said Fenton quickly.

"They'll respect my credentials. It's part of their business to," de Vaudois said. "Your offense is serious: climbing at night in military territory without a *laisser passer*. An international violation of law, in present terms. I'll report it by telephone to headquarters——"

"To your sister in Geneva?" said Fenton, her hands in her pockets still, and de Vaudois smiled.

"It's past midnight," he said. He had glanced at the watch on his wrist, and now he shook the sleeve of his overcoat down. "Now that we understand each other, we'll be off," he said. As she turned toward the dark of the hallway, she saw him drop his right hand into his pocket onto the weapon he carried there. "You'll walk straight to the front door and out it," he said. "I'll follow exactly two steps behind you, which means that the rope remains taut between us. Go quietly and there won't be any trouble. If you cry out and there's interference, I warn you I'll shoot instantly," he said.

On the way down, she was thinking as they moved the length of the hall together, *on the way down, I must find the means to bring it to an end. He's not a mountain man, he doesn't know the path and the turnings of it. To take it slowly, carefully,* she thought as she moved down the hall before him; *to plan for the break, not to hurry, not to fumble the moment when it will come.* Here was the cobbler's corner where, before you started across the ice in the years of peace,

187

you could have your worn nailheads replaced in the tough soles of your shoes. Here was the counter where the souvenirs and postcards—the miniature alpenstocks, the edelweiss pasted to colored views of the mountains—had been on display. Here was the case where the climbing medals had lain on purple velvet, and the glass balls encasing a puny Mont Blanc or a statue of the Virgin had waited to be shaken until the mock snow fell deep and white inside. Here was the rack for the canes, and here the chair that Bastineau had run against as they came in, recognized as she passed them in darkness. She had reached the door, and she opened it now, and de Vaudois was close behind her. *To move slowly, carefully,* she thought. *Not to fail them. Not to act in panic before the instant has come.*

"Go straight out, and then wait," said de Vaudois. "I'm going to lock the door behind us. Then you'll lead me to the window ledge where the key remains. I want everything left in the usual order, in case anyone comes to investigate," he said.

Fenton went through the doorway, and down the step, and there she halted, the rope twisted tight above her hips. And then she became aware of the other presence. It was there in the cold and the dark on the platform of land before her—not movement, not so much as the sound of breathing —but she knew beyond any question that someone was waiting in the silence there.

"Very well. Now the window," de Vaudois said, and Fenton turned, and the rope was taut between them as she led him the few steps to the ledge. "Very well. It's done," said de Vaudois. "Now we'll go down. We'll go," he repeated, but Fenton stood motionless on the stone.

"I'm not sure of the direction," she said, and she waited, her eyes strained wide in the darkness—and then the unseen man before them spoke aloud.

"So this is your place of rendezvous!" his voice said in contempt across the dark.

"Ah, Jacqueminot, Jacqueminot!" Fenton said, scarcely aloud. And then her voice rose clearer. "Jacqueminot, he must be stopped—he must be stopped—he has spied on us——"

"Silence," said de Vaudois quietly behind her. "I have you covered," he said.

"Then shoot!" said Jacqueminot in the same low, bitter voice. "One shot fired here would be heard up to the highest Cols, and even beyond them! The rocks would echo so loud with it that every man on the frontier would take it for the signal and start down!"

"I do not wish to spread an alarm," said de Vaudois. "Moreover, I would prefer that we parted as friends——"

"Friends!" cried Jacqueminot, and she heard him say the word of blasphemy beneath his breath, and the leather of his rusksack's harness creaked as he came nearer to them. "You both were to have left Truex today—that was the story you told," he said. "And I find you here at the glacier tonight!"

"Oh, come! This is too bad," said de Vaudois almost pleasantly. "Here are the three of us again—faceless, formless, ageless, without starting place or destination, in precisely the same situation as when we met that first night on the train. Again we are merely three voices exchanging words, completely unknown to one another! In darkness we met, and it is only fitting that we part in darkness. You'll excuse us if we say good night to you, *monsieur*. I, at least, am feeling the chill of the evening and am anxious to get down———"

"When I traveled with you in the train that night, I didn't suspect!" said Jacqueminot, and he might have been speaking to Fenton alone, saying it to her quickly and bitterly. "I believed you were strangers to each other—but in the days that followed there were things that put me on my guard. And now I see it! Tonight, whatever you're up to, neither of you is going down!"

"That's where you're wrong," said de Vaudois, and his voice was pleasant still. "*Mademoiselle*, may I ask you kindly to lead the way?"

Fenton felt the rope tauten between them, and she braced herself against the traction of it. *Now*, she thought, *now, however it ends for me, it is the moment to speak.*

"Jacqueminot!" she cried out. "Stop him—he has everything—the names—*combines*———" And as the shot sang past her, Jacqueminot leapt forward in the darkness, and she was jerked backward by the rope as he struck de Vaudois the first sharp, quick blow. For the brief time it endured, she was part of the two men's struggle, part of the scuffling, and the gasping for breath, of the low and savage cursing, of the skidding of nails on the terrace's stone. And then the second shot rang out, and the movement ceased, and Fenton crouched trembling there an instant. It was only when the rope jerked at her waist again that she put out her hand and groped for life in the darkness. After a moment, she found the bare throat of the man who had fallen to the ground. Her fingers moved in terror to the clothing—*the stuff of the overcoat*, she thought; *the velvet collar, or else the flannel shirt and the wind jacket's tissue*—and here they touched the wind jacket's stuff, and here the rucksack's strap slipped from the shoulder, and "Jacqueminot, Jacqueminot!" she cried aloud.

"Get up," said de Vaudois in a fierce whisper behind her now. "Get up and start walking—quick!"

Fenton got to her feet, and her heart had gone wild in her breast, and her teeth were shaking as if from the cold.

"So that's the way you do it—so that's the way you kill them!" she cried out. "You—you men of the world—cultured—civilized—velvet collars on your coats!" In a moment she knew she would start beating him, striking him hard and wildly with her hands.

"Start walking!" said de Vaudois quickly across the darkness, and he jerked the rope between them. "Get going fast!"

"I won't go a step with you!" Fenton cried. "You'll see to Jacqueminot! If they've heard two shots above to warn them, then let them hear a third!" She clenched her shaking hands by her sides, and she swung around to face him. "You'll make a light——"

She heard the grunt of air from the expired lungs, as if de Vaudois had stepped upon the fallen body in his haste, and then his open hand struck hard across her mouth.

"He's dead, you fool!" said de Vaudois between his teeth. "Now walk! There's been enough interference! I want to get down fast."

She began to walk as if in a dream now, crossed the platform of land, moved toward the smell and life of vegetation, while the barren world of rock and ice died quietly behind. The cold of the night was nothing, and the dark nothing, and she did not feel the bite of the rope at her waist, but she walked in dazed, speechless bewilderment before him, taking in automatic infallibility the path of the descent. *If I had left Truex this afternoon*, it went in endless repetition, *Jacqueminot would not be lying dead before the door. If I had left Truex this afternoon, he would be crossing the glaciers now, and de Vaudois would know nothing. I have betrayed them—Frenchmen, rebels, patriots. If I had left Truex——*

"Faster!" said de Vaudois behind her, and the rope pulled savagely at her waist. *If I can go slowly enough*, she thought, *they may overtake us from above. Two shots to warn them——* "Faster!" cried de Vaudois, and he was sliding and slipping over the rocks and roots of the pathway, panting with effort as he came.

I can take the wrong turning, lose him here in the forest, the rush of words went on in tumult. *If he shoots me for it as he shot Jacqueminot, then that is the way it must be.*

"Keep going!" de Vaudois cried out, and his lungs were gasping for breath now. "Go faster! I've used the gun once, I can use it again!" he said.

But the letter, the letter! her heart cried out in anguish. *If I do not get down alive, the letter he left with Madame Perrin will go across the frontier! For one more agent lost in the mountains, Jeanne-Marie and Père Chatelard and*

192

monsieur le curé will perish! Cousin Perrin and La Cousine and Dizot and Falcroz will stand with their hands tied behind them against a prison wall! I cannot die until the letter has been taken from Madame Perrin's hands!

"Faster!" cried de Vaudois, whining the words through his teeth, and now Fenton began to run, sliding quickly down under the needled boughs of the trees.

To take the wrong turning then, she thought, *lead him down past the farm instead of to Truex, and once within earshot, cry out Cousin Perrin's name! Cry out,* she thought in desperation as she ran, *and have the pistol speak again! Cry out, and have Cousin Perrin fling wide the farmhouse door and stand there against the light, so that de Vaudois can take careful aim! Not that, not that—but lead him to Cousin Perrin's door, without his knowing——*

"Keep going! Run, I tell you!" de Vaudois said, and he jerked the rope at her waist.

Here was the break in the path and the trees, and Fenton swung quickly to the left, and de Vaudois followed blindly where she led. Because they were lower now, there was little snow left on the forest floor, and the clatter and slide of their nailed boots was like the panic of horses pounding down the trail.

"Which way will the lights of the village be?" asked de Vaudois, and his breath was crying for succor. "It can't be far now. Which direction does the village lie?"

"At this hour, there wouldn't be lights," said Fenton.

"Don't slow down! Keep going!" de Vaudois cried out. "We don't know who's behind us!"

On the opening slope below them she could see the shape of the farmhouse roof, and the wooden chimney's high, square turret darker against the darkness of the sky. And now their feet struck pasture land, and she could hear the sound of the water dripping, not stopped by the night's cold yet but falling slowly into the cattle trough before the farmhouse door. They were crossing the bare ground that lay before the house itself, their shoes striking the ruts that cattle hoofs had carved in the frozen mud, and de Vaudois was breathing heavily as he came.

"Where are we?" de Vaudois said, and his voice was wary.

"I don't understand it," said Fenton. "I must have lost the footpath——"

They were wading through knee-high vegetation now, splintering twigs and undergrowth beneath their feet, and de Vaudois jerked her to a halt.

"That's a lie," he said. "You're deliberately trying—— Here," he said, and the rope moved savagely. "I could do as well as this myself! Turn around!" he said. "You follow me——"

And then, as he took the next two, fumbling steps, she heard the other thing—the snap of steel in the darkness, and his furious cry of pain.

"Don't move, don't speak," he said, the sound of it twisted in his mouth. "Something's got me. My foot," he said. "I'll need help to get me free."

"A trap?" said Fenton, and she did not move. And then, as if Cousin Perrin's voice had actually spoken to her in the dark, she heard him say again as he had said it in the storeroom beneath the cattle's stalls: *We are protected . . . it would not be wise to wander in the brush around the farm. . . .*

"We must be close to a farmhouse. They've set it here for some kind of beast," he said, speaking scarcely above a whisper, and now the dogs within had begun to bark aloud. "They're coming to open the door!" said de Vaudois fiercely across the dark. "You know the role you have to play! Whoever it is, we got lost in the mountains this afternoon together. Nothing has happened. We have not been as high as the Mer de Glace. We have seen no one. We merely want to get back to the village." She heard the groan of pain through his teeth now. "I have my hand on my gun still. No trickery," he said.

And now the door of the farmhouse opened, and the dogs ran out in fury to them, and Cousin Perrin stood in his night-shirt on the threshold, his black hat on his head, a lantern lifted in one hand.

"Back, cretins! Here, imbeciles!" he called out to the dogs which cringed snarling and muttering at Fenton's and de Vaudois' feet. "*B'en,* I thought I heard the trap go, and I said: 'I've got my fox now.' I didn't think it would be humans," he said, and he held the lantern higher so that it might shed its light upon their faces below him in the dark.

"Get down here and open it!" de Vaudois said through his teeth. "It's got me across the instep. Open it quick!"

"*B'en,* it's Mademoiselle Ravel," said Cousin Perrin, speaking slowly, musingly from the doorway. "I was in two minds about setting that trap tonight," he said. "Fox been around here after the chickens as regularly as the Boche com-

195

mission. I wouldn't know which to say takes the most fowl, fox or Boche," he said, and he spat on the ground.

"I'm caught—do you understand me?" cried de Vaudois. "Get it off me!"

"*B'en*, the key's hanging up somewhere inside the house," said Cousin Perrin, and he stood on the step still with the lantern in his hand. "But I said to myself that as long as La Cousine was down in the village watching over the dead to-night, I'd set the trap. You can't tell what might be wandering around a farmhouse at night since they've taken over the country." He turned without haste on the threshold, and the light went with him as he walked into the house again. Ring by ring it receded as he made his way through the entry where the Virgin stood in her niche with the deathless flowers before her, wave by quivering, shallow wave it ebbed until they were left in darkness again. It was ten minutes before Cousin Perrin appeared again, and in that time de Vaudois had not spoken, but Fenton heard the sobbing and cursing of his breath behind her in the night. "*B'en*, thought I might as well put some clothing on before I came out in the cold," said Cousin Perrin, and Fenton saw in the lantern's light that he was dressed now. "Catch a lumbago in November, and you're crippled the winter," he said.

"You took the time—you took the time to put your clothes on—while I—I——" de Vaudois was saying, and now he cursed him, his voice like the snarl of an animal, caught and frenzied with pain.

"*B'en*, a lumbago'll get you in your nightshirt, and you won't be able to move for a week," said Cousin Perrin. He set the lantern down beside de Vaudois on the frozen soil, and as he stooped above him, Fenton saw the gleam of malice and humor in Cousin Perrin's eye. "If it had been a fox, I'd have had him good," he said. "The trap was rusty, but it's bitten nicely into the bone. Broken the instep, I should say. You won't be walking for a while now."

It was five minutes before he had the foot free of the trap, and then he helped de Vaudois into the entryway and bade him lean against the wall while he called the dogs in and locked the door against the night. In the kitchen, he placed a chair for him near the hearth, and de Vaudois sank down in pain and exhaustion on it, one hand in his overcoat pocket still, the incongruously cocky hat upon his head. Because of the rope that hung between them, Fenton could not move across the room, and she stood near the hearth, with her head turned from him, breathing the good smell of the cattle in. Cousin Perrin had hooked the lantern to the beam above the table in the corner, and now he took the bottle of cognac down from the shelf.

"Take a swallow of this, and you'll be a man again," he said. He held the glass of it out to the man slumped in the chair before him, and de Vaudois took it in his left hand and drank it quickly down.

"Have you antiseptics in the house?" he asked, but Cousin Perrin might not have heard the question, for he did not answer but kneeled down by the bed of ashes on the hearth and laid the dry bouquets of brush lightly in. In a moment, a delicate spiral of milky smoke rose from the scarcely glowing dust, drawn upward into the chimney's tall, tapering avenue that stood open above their heads. As the little wings of fire sprang to life, Cousin Perrin reached up for the iron arm and pulled the caldron into place above the growing flame. "This wound has got to be sterilized. It's got to be done now, before poisoning sets in," said de Vaudois, and his voice was stronger, sharper.

"*B'en,* we'll have the water boiling in an hour or two," said Cousin Perrin. He was standing now, his eyes on the rope that hung slack from the double loop around Fenton's waist, following the twist of it to de Vaudois' chair.

"We've been wandering around since it got dark—lost the way," said Fenton, and she shivered a little. "We roped ourselves so as to keep close to each other——"

"It's a queer enough way you're roped," said Cousin Perrin, and he forced his blunt fingers in under the cord at her waist. "Whoever's done it, it's been fixed so you couldn't get free." And *Cousin Perrin, Cousin Perrin,* said her eyes in desperation on him, *his hand's on a gun in his pocket or else I'd cry out the truth to you, Cousin Perrin! He has a list of the men in Lyon, he has an official report on the village, he's an agent—he will wipe out the heart of Truex if he lives!* Cousin Perrin stood gravely watching her from under the brim of his hat, as if summoning her to speak aloud, but because her lips were silent, he turned now to de Vaudois' chair. "There's no need to be roped in here," he said.

"Leave it," said de Vaudois when he saw the other man's hand on the rope. "There are more urgent things than that to see to. I need a doctor. I need him at once. Lockjaw—I'm in danger of lockjaw with a wound from a trap set in a barnyard like that. Any doctor can tell you that manure in a foot wound——" His eyes were on his foot before him, and the blood clotting now across the shattered bone.

"*B'en,* the doctor of Truex, he's gone the way of all good patriots long ago," said Cousin Perrin, and he stooped to lay more wood in on the flame.

"There's Dizot, the bonesetter," de Vaudois said, and his voice was sharp.

"He's watching the body in the crypt tonight with La Cousine," said Cousin Perrin almost lazily.

And *There must be a way to speak out now!* thought Fenton. She looked quickly from one man's face to the other, and she thrust her hands in her pockets to hide their agitation there.

"You will have to get me a doctor. Do you understand me?" de Vaudois was saying. He leaned forward from his chair toward Cousin Perrin, and the scar was as white as wax across his face. "Lockjaw—I'm in danger of lockjaw," he said, and his right hand was in his overcoat pocket still. "I'll pay high if you'll get me a doctor here. Money," he said, and he made the gesture with his thumb and forefinger. "You can name your price," he said.

"*B'en,* there's only *monsieur le curé* to give the injections since the doctor's gone," said Cousin Perrin slowly. "They call him in for all kinds and sorts of cases now—childbirth, snakebite, scaldings," he said, and slowly he shifted his black hat on his head.

"Then you will get the curé," said de Vaudois, and his voice was tense. "You'll go down the mountain now and get him."

"*B'en*, I've never yet taken orders from anyone in my own house," said Cousin Perrin, and he said it quietly, deliberately. "Nor have I ever left the farm alone at night, with the livestock and a fire in it, and I won't be starting now," he said.

"There's Mademoiselle Ravel," said de Vaudois, trying to say it with patience to him. "She'll stay here and see there's no trouble. She'll tend to my foot when the water has boiled——"

"May the heavens fall and the rivers rise and submerge us if *mademoiselle* should ever kneel down and wash a stranger's foot!" Cousin Perrin cried aloud. "No! I stay here in this house, under my own roof, and *mademoiselle* will go down to the village and get some sleep in bed! I'll do for your foot tonight, and when La Cousine comes up the hill in the morning, there'll be time enough to fetch the curé or chemist——"

Cousin Perrin turned and laid his hands on the rope now, but de Vaudois spoke sharply from his chair.

"Don't touch the rope, if you please," he said, and Cousin Perrin glanced at him from under his hat brim, but his hands did not falter. "Stand back!" said de Vaudois, and his voice and his eyes were violent. "I'll not be interfered with," he said.

Fenton saw the thing move in his pocket, saw it jerk forward, and the blunt nose of it take shape against the pocket's cloth.

"Cousin Perrin, he's armed! There's a gun in his hand!" she cried out, and now she was between them. "Cousin Perrin, go quickly—the village—get the letter from Madame Perrin

—destroy it——" and de Vaudois whipped the pistol from his pocket and she faced the black, evil muzzle of it in that instant before the final crash would come. "The letter—destroy it——" she cried out again, and *Now it will come, now is the moment,* she thought in anguish, *and I am a coward, I cannot take it with the eyes uncovered as the hostages do. Now it will come,* she thought, and she covered her face with her hands, but even as she did it, she heard the other thing, wondrous and loud and wild. *"L'Infant'rie Alpin-e, voilà mes amours!"* it came, shouted down as if from the mountain heights through the tough, cupped palms of a mountaineer.

Her hands dropped from her face, and in the instant before de Vaudois fired at her, he looked above his head and gave a cry of fear. Easily, gracefully as a jumper on skis, Bastineau came down the chimney's broad, wooden shaft, his arms spread like a diver's, his eyes and teeth pure white and savage in his face. And then he was on de Vaudois' head and shoulders, his knees locked around him, the heel of one boot cracking the right wrist so that the shot went wild across the kitchen, and the two men crashed from the chair to the floor. Fenton was jerked from her feet with the force of it, pulled to her knees by the rope around her waist still, and Cousin Perrin sprang forward and held her shoulders in his hard, blunt hands, watching, sharp-eyed, the two men struggling on the hearth.

"Quick! The gun!" Fenton cried out to him, but it was already in Bastineau's fingers. He was lying, nearly prone, upon de Vaudois, one knee bearing his full weight on him, and there was no sound, except for the gasp for breath in the two men's throats, as he lifted the gun and fired it twice into de Vaudois' heart. Then he stood up, and he did not speak for a moment, but he wiped the palms of his hands off on the sides of his dark knickerbockers, wiped them slowly, carefully, automatically.

"So—vengeance," he said after a little. There was nothing but the muttering of the dogs around the body to be heard in the room. "Jacqueminot——" he began, and he looked at Fenton.

"Up there—in front of the Montanvert," she said.

"I came back off the glacier when I heard the two shots. I found him," he said, and it may have been tears that were grinding at his jaws. But his eyes fell on the rope hanging slack from her waist, and at once he snapped the knife from his pocket. "Here. Let's be finished with this one," he said, and then he stopped short. "And you—did he harm you?"

"No, nothing," said Fenton, but Bastineau's eyes were on her face.

"There's a mark across your cheek, your mouth," he said.

"He followed me up. He was there from the beginning—listening to us!" she said. "He had all the information written down. Everything. If I hadn't gone up like a fool tonight—then Jacqueminot—none of this——" She stopped in grief.

"You came up because I asked you to," said Bastineau. He had the blade on the rope now, but Cousin Perrin stopped him with one stubborn hand.

"*B'en*, you can't cut a rope like that—not a rope as good as that one, Bastineau," he said. "Every mountaineer would turn over in his grave."

"Undo it from his waist, then," Bastineau said. "I'm through now. You were so careful to lock the door that I had to come down the chimney after him. I'm going to wash my hands clean of him in the cattle room," he said.

It was Cousin Perrin who unknotted the rope from the dead man's waist, and who wound it now, coil by coil, loop by loop, carefully in his hands. When he had come to where Fenton stood, he halted and loosened the double coil from her hips, and slipped it to the floor. And now she was free, and she stepped from the fallen ring of it, and crossed, a little unsteadily, to the table under the lantern's light. Cousin Perrin was done with the winding of the rope, and he hung it respectfully on the cheese-room door, and then he turned and he took the dead man by the sleeves of his elegant, city overcoat, and he dragged him from the hearth and across the kitchen flaggings, and out of the door into the entryway. Then he came back in silence and stooped to the fire, and he laid fresh wood in on the flame.

"Because you came to the Montanvert, we got de Vaudois," Bastineau said as he swung abruptly down on the bench beside her. His face was gleaming and cold with water, and his hands were as clean as timber stripped of its bark. "If you had left Truex this afternoon," he said, "he would still be alive to go back and tell them what he'd found here." He sat looking at the side of her face as he talked, and because of the despair in her heart she could not turn and meet his eyes. "He struck you. There's still the mark of it," he said, and his fingers touched her lips for an instant, and she felt the tears rise, weak and hot, within her. "Cousin Perrin!" Bastineau called out across the room. "Could we have a drink of *pinard*? And if there's a piece or two of bread and cheese to *casser la croûte*? I've got to get up the mountain faster than I came down."

Cousin Perrin opened the cupboard door then, and he brought the glasses and the bottle of red wine to them, and he set the quarter wheel of good bread on the table.

"The goat cheese is fresh," he said, and he came back with the dish of it, and set it down.

"There's a group coming through tonight, by the Col des Hirondelles," Bastineau said, and he poured the wine and cut the bread for Fenton. "I'm late, but they'll wait for me," he said. "Drink quickly, you're tired. Eat this," he said, and he put the dark-crusted bread and the white cheese in her hand. "There'll be five escaped prisoners with the others— Frenchmen coming home, and Jeanne-Marie's man among them," he said, and he might have been speaking to Cousin Perrin of something as usual as the weather, or of how deep the snow might fall.

"So Besnard's coming through?" said Cousin Perrin. He sat at the table with them, but he did not take a glass and drink. "*B'en*, Jeanne-Marie deserves it. She's waited like a widow. Three years she's been saying nothing, but waited dry-eyed for the sight of him," he said.

And *What am I to do now?* said Fenton in silence, and because he had given the wine to her, she drank it down. *What can I do now but seek to lift my head in pride instead of hanging it in shame because of the pitiful limits that I set to love? What can I do now?* she thought, and she set her teeth against

204

the taste of crying. *Jeanne-Marie, teach me to be strong, to go back to Lyon like a woman of dignity and courage*—and suddenly the course of it altered, swift as the crack of a sail in a changing wind, and she jumped to her feet before them.

"The letter! There is still the letter to be stopped!" she cried out. "The names of the partisans—the sources of food supplies—the report to headquarters——" she began, and then stopped abruptly, for the knocking was sounding on the outer door.

"*B'en*, it might be the gendarmes come up to call," said Cousin Perrin slowly after a moment, and he ordered the dogs to quiet. "They wouldn't like the sight of a dead man lying there," he said. He got to his feet, and he looked down at Bastineau seated at the table, eating the bread and cheese still, and drinking the red wine down. "There's the storeroom under the last goat's stall. The two of you better keep out of sight——"

But a hand tapped at the little window now where the twisted geranium stalks stood in the tins, and they saw the high beak of *monsieur le curé*'s nose, and the white of his brows in the dark outside the pane. Bastineau leapt to his feet, and ran light as a cat through the entryway, and they heard him unlock the door to him, and if he and the curé spoke of the dead man lying on the flaggings as they came through, their words were brief, for they came at once into the kitchen's light.

"It's not often you come so high, *mon père*," said Cousin Perrin. "Sit here by the fire," he said, and he set the chair for him, but the curé did not sit down.

"There'll be time enough for resting, an eternity of it," he

205

said then, and Bastineau took the cloak from his shoulders. "With the news I have tonight," said the curé in his strong, ringing voice, "I am no longer an old man, and I stand! I have come up from the village as fast as you could, Bastineau —I came running like a young man! I could not stay in the rectory alone with it—I woke Jeanne-Marie Favret and Père Chatelard and Falcroz in their beds to tell them before I left Truex!" He stood with his arms opened wide in exultation to them, his lean hands quivering with eagerness and joy. "Tonight—just tonight—the news came through from Radio-Boston. The Americans have landed in North Africa!" he said.

"The Americans, the Americans!" Fenton repeated, scarcely aloud, and she looked in wonder at him across the room. He had put his arms around Bastineau's shoulders, and, like father and son, they embraced in emotion and salute.

"For two days the BBC has been blotted out by interference," the curé said, and he and Bastineau came to the table now, their arms around each other, and they sat down facing Fenton under the lantern's light. "London and Boston both indistinct since forty-eight hours, tuned out by the Germans," he said, and Cousin Perrin sat down on the bench beside him, harking to him, and his tears were falling. Cousin Perrin's tears were falling shamelessly onto the backs of his own tough, workworn hands. "Tonight I got one or two sentences clearly —150,000 men—the British fleet—the Americans have taken Algiers!" the curé said in triumph. "They are marching on Oran!" he said.

"*B'en,* start your men marching down the other side of the

pass tonight, Bastineau!" Cousin Perrin said, and he wiped his nose with the side of his hand. "Start them down, Bastineau," he said in pride, "so that they'll be there to join up with the Americans when they reach Italian soil!"

"But there's this," said the curé in warning, his eyes brilliant in his frail, high-boned face. "The Germans are pouring down across France. They've reached Lyon already. There is no longer the Occupied and the Unoccupied Zones—the line of demarcation has been abolished. It's the whole of France invaded——"

"Then our men coming through from Switzerland tonight —they can't go farther," said Bastineau.

"They'll stay and wait for orders with the rest of you here," the curé said.

"You, Fenton," said Bastineau quickly, and he looked at her across the table's boards. "Lyon occupied—you can't go back——"

"Then I'll stay here," said Fenton quietly. "The thing we have prayed on our knees for has begun, and I shall be here to take part in it," she said.

"But here?" Bastineau began, and then he reached out his hand across the table to her. "How could you live here?" he asked.

"Live?" she cried out in rebuke to him, and she did not touch his hand. "How have the other women of Europe lived? Did they lose their courage and die in the years of starvation and hopelessness and grief? When their men came back they were there, women still, waiting to hold them in their arms!" She dropped her eyes from his face, but her voice went on speaking quietly to him. "Or if I am not to live here as a woman, then I could live here as Jacqueminot did. I brought him to his death, and he died believing the lowest, the bitterest thing possible of me. If I could take his place, it might be some sort of retribution—it might in the end be some sort of explanation to him," she said.

"His place," said Bastineau, repeating it softly, and then he put the thought of it aside. "You could collect the wool, carry it, see to the working of it, but the rest of it—no. There's no place above for a woman. There's only hardship, hunger, men alone——"

"*B'en*, she could do it as your wife," said Cousin Perrin, slowly, almost lazily.

"My wife——" said Bastineau, and then he turned to the curé and looked at him strangely, shyly, in wonder.

"The Germans will have reached Truex by tomorrow. I can marry you here tonight," the curé said.

And now Bastineau swung himself up from the bench and across the timber of the table, and he sat down swiftly beside Fenton.

"No roof over my head, no money, nothing to call my own," he began it quickly, in something like desperation to her. "Your husband—even as your husband I go up the Col des Hirondelles tonight and get the men across it——"

"Yes," said Fenton, "yes," and her eyes moved on his face before her, touching the silky brows, and the hair springing back from his forehead; seeing the clear white teeth, and the deep sweet lines of the sun and the weather at his eyes and mouth. "Yes, Bastineau. Yes, Bastineau," she said.

"*B'en,* after standing up as witness for you, I'll go down the hill and call on the hotelkeeper before the Boches get up from the valley," said Cousin Perrin. "If she's sent off the letter, I'll get it from Gustav at the post office itself. It'll be a chance to start saying the *bon jour* to them," he said.

"Come," said the curé. "Take off your hat, then, Cousin Perrin."

"My hat?" said Cousin Perrin, and in sudden outrage he touched the black felt brim of it, and then he bowed his head and meekly took it from his brow.

"Come," said *monsieur le curé* to them again, and he crossed to the hearth to warm his hands at the fire an instant. "This is just the beginning for all of us," he said.

A NOTE ABOUT THE AUTHOR

Kay Boyle was born in St. Paul, Minnesota, in 1903, and married a Frenchman and went to France in 1922. She has lived in France, England, and Austria since then, returning to America in 1941. She is the author of thirteen books: *Wedding Day; Plagued by the Nightingale; Year Before Last; The First Lover; Gentlemen, I Address You Privately; My Next Bride; The White Horses of Vienna; Death of a Man; A Glad Day; The Youngest Camel; Monday Night; The Crazy Hunter;* and *Primer for Combat.* She has twice won the O. Henry Memorial Prize for the best short story of the year, and in 1934 was awarded a Guggenheim Fellowship.